T0001921

Helga's
Amazing Life

HELGA'S AMAZING LIFE

Tinmouth Pond Series Book 4

AUSTIN BURBANK

TATE PUBLISHING
AND ENTERPRISES, LLC

Helga's Amazing Life
Copyright © 2016 by Austin Burbank. All rights reserved.

No part of this publication may be reproduced, stored in a retrieval system or transmitted in any way by any means, electronic, mechanical, photocopy, recording or otherwise without the prior permission of the author except as provided by USA copyright law.

This novel is a work of fiction. Names, descriptions, entities, and incidents included in the story are products of the author's imagination. Any resemblance to actual persons, events, and entities is entirely coincidental.

The opinions expressed by the author are not necessarily those of Tate Publishing, LLC.

Published by Tate Publishing & Enterprises, LLC
127 E. Trade Center Terrace | Mustang, Oklahoma 73064 USA
1.888.361.9473 | www.tatepublishing.com

Tate Publishing is committed to excellence in the publishing industry. The company reflects the philosophy established by the founders, based on Psalm 68:11,

"The Lord gave the word and great was the company of those who published it."

Book design copyright © 2016 by Tate Publishing, LLC. All rights reserved.
Cover design by Bill Francis Peralta
Interior design by Manolito Bastasa

Published in the United States of America

ISBN: 978-1-68270-764-7
1. Fiction / Fantasy / General
2. Fiction / Fairy Tales, Folk Tales, Legends & Mythology
16.03.04

ACKNOWLEDGMENTS

I want to acknowledge some of the people whom I have encountered, who walked with me, and who still have relationships with me who have either became a part of a character in my books, given rise to a character, or helped trigger a storyline.

To the Chrises who have been part of my authorship experience. Chris Miller, who sat on the edge of Tinmouth Pond with me one evening when I said, "There must be a monster in there somewhere, Chris. There's a monster in every pond in Vermont." Chris agreed, and the stories began. Chris Giddings, a longtime friend. Christina Kumka, who wrote an article about me, and I asked if she would like to be a character in a book. Of course she agreed to be a character.

To my aunt Thelma for letting me use her name for a fun character. The character is no resemblance to my aunt, I want to add. Thelma, I hope you like the story.

To Bruce, the best veterinarian in the world, for agreeing to be a basis for a character in this book. The fun part of writing is to create characters and giving them life through their actions and adventures.

To Mr. Baker for the use of his logging truck in this book. (I told you I would put you in the acknowledgment.)

And to the muse that wakes me up at 4:00 a.m. with the next chapter of the story and answers to questions I had already written. This experience has surprised me more than anyone. Thank you to my muse.

If you see a part of yourself in any of my books, it is probably because we are made up of multipersonalities and everyone has many facets that look like the person sitting beside you. I hope you do see yourself somewhere in my books, and I hope that my stories bring back memories and thoughts and feelings. I hope these emotions, memories, and thoughts improve your life immediately. Longlost forgotten memories are the very best.

Surprise yourself each and every day. Make life worth living.

CHAPTER ONE

This was the worse monsoon season that anyone in China under the age of thirty had ever experienced.

There I was, riding in a third-rate taxi, travelling on some of the most devastated roads in China. Being from Vermont, I knew bad roads, especially the ones with the signs that read "Frost Heaves Ahead." These Chinese roads were ten times worse.

I reached down and tightened my seat belt, not for fear of being thrown from the taxi—that fear had alluded me twenty miles back—but to affix myself to the seat to stop my head from headbanging the side door window. I wondered if I'd realize I had a concussion if I had one.

Only two weeks ago, I was sitting in the editor's office of the *Tinmouth Gazette* when Mr. Moneybags, as I refer to the owner of the paper behind his back, told me that I was headed to China for an exclusive event. He rattled on about an ol' college chum or army buddy, I really wasn't listening because I really didn't care; I was just waiting for the weekend to arrive. But then he said, "My friend got the Chinese government to allow one non-Asian to visit and photograph the world's richest jade mine. No American had ever been close to this mine," he continued with hand gestures. "The Chinese government decided that the mine needed to be listed on the world's list of greatest wonders. My friend called and said that if I had a journalist who would cover the mine story with the utmost respect and dignity for the Chinese government and the Chinese people, he would make it happen."

Mr. Moneybags paused and looked over his bifocals directly at me.

"You mean you want me to cover the story?" I asked. "What about pictures?"

"Chris, you are my first choice," he replied. "And you get a total of twelve photos that will be exported with the approval of the Chinese government. This is a chance of a lifetime!"

"I'll do it. When do I leave?"

"Your flight leaves New York City in two days," he said as he leaned back in his oversized leather chair.

The rest of the conversation was about logistics and protocol. What to do where and when as not to upset or offend the Chinese officials.

Forty-eight hours later, I sat on the plane waiting for take off to my first real photojournalist assignment of my career. Guess that college education was worth the money after all.

The flight had a lot of turbulence due to the bad weather that had encircled the globe. I was never so glad to be on solid ground as I was when the plane finally taxied on Chinese soil. It was a frightening ride.

The destruction and devastation that Mother Nature can unleash with a monsoon is unbelievable. What nature can do with water and energy is just amazing.

The Chinese people had lost many dams, most roads had been damaged, crops were lost, and there were deaths of citizens and animals. The monsoon had crossed China with an angry force. The force of unexpected rushing water had caught many small remote villages unprepared, and many lives were lost.

So there I was in China, in the middle of the monsoon season, in a dirty taxi, in the middle of the night, headed to who knew where.

The clouds were black and billowing earthward, pouring millions of gallons of rain onto an already saturated land. The mountains in the distance were as black as the clouds and appeared even more threatening. Everything was dark and depressing. I opened my laptop, producing the only light in the backseat. The car's dashboard lights illuminated the driver. He had a strange blue glow about him. I had already gone through two auxiliary batteries that I had brought with me, and I hadn't seen any place to plug in my charging station. My solar-powered charger didn't make it on my flight. It was probably headed to New Zealand, if not to Sweden.

I was reviewing some information that I had downloaded about Chinese politics when my screen slowly faded to black. "Oh great. Now the battery is dead. My only working battery is *dead*," I said out loud as I closed my case and cinched the seat belt even tighter. I leaned back against the protruding springs of the old seat and watched the back of the driver's head bobbing as we continued the trip to the mountains.

I graduated with a major in English with concentrated studies in mythology and legends. I concluded in my own mind that myths were man's stories used to control the masses. Legends, as far as I could figure out, were the stories of people who had hallucinations after injuries or ingesting something poisonous. Both story lines had no inclusion in my story of the jade mine.

A story of a jade mine in China. Not the kind of assignment that would be winning me a Pulitzer Prize anytime soon, I thought to myself.

The old taxi driver drove for hours in the pouring rain; then we finally reached some treeless foothills. The driver stopped the vehicle, got out, and opened the trunk and then opened my door. He handed me my carry-on bag and pointed to a dark metal gate set into the hillside. I walked in the drizzling rain toward the gate and watched as the taxi drove away. This was the first time in my life that I felt totally alone and helpless. As I approached the double gates, the gates opened as if they were expecting me, a stranger in a strange land in an even stranger situation. Two Chinese men in matching emerald-green coats with gold braids greeted me. They had a recent photo of me so they could identify me as the foreigner that they were waiting for. One man took my carry-on and the other man took my computer. I was left with my camera, paper, and pencils.

They marched, and I followed them into the mountain. We walked and we walked. "Where are we going?" I asked, but of course they didn't understand English. What was I thinking?

We reached a set of huge antique doors with delicately carved hardware, probably cast a hundred years before Columbus discovered North America.

The doors swung open, and the three of us stepped into the most valuable jade mine on the face of the earth.

My heart stopped. Every nerve in my body tingled as I looked at the most beautiful thing that I had ever envisioned. I had never seen anything like it. The mine was cavernous in its size, and it possessed the largest natural formation of mutton fat jade known to man. Mutton fat jade is the most valuable jade in the world.

The most-prized pieces of mutton fat jade had been removed for the emperor. Workers for hundreds of years had carved out this most amazing shrine. It was a palace of beautifully marbleized jade. It was miraculous, it was stunning, and it was exhilarating. The entire mine was completely carved. There were stairways, columns, rooms of every size and shape, and all of it was magically lit from behind. The entire mine had a soft glow that I had never seen before. There were hand-carved Buddhas on every ledge and in every crevice. Each one more beautiful than the one before it. In each corner, there were monstrous fire-breathing jade dragons standing guard. They appeared so lifelike that I was afraid their flames would scorch the ceiling.

An altar protecting jade-encrusted urns hung from the ceiling in the middle of the room. Beautiful, just amazingly beautiful.

I was the first and only non-Asian to have ever seen this spectacular space. Only the emperor, his family, and the workers who labored in this mine had ever seen this special wonder of the world, and I had only twelve photo opportunities to show the outside world this amazing place.

I held up my new camera directly over my head and took my first shot. This is the first camera that I had ever seen that is capable of taking a 360-degree picture, which is technically only one photograph.

Everything in this mine is intricately carved white jade except for a small bank of vertical steel bars some twenty feet above the mine's floor.

I desperately hoped that my photographs would expertly express the beauty of this secret place. I hope my words will be able to describe what I am feeling in this very spiritual setting.

"I am sure you have many questions," an Asian man said in perfect English as he walked up behind me. He was a mature man, wrinkled skin scorched by the sun with a long, well-shaped beard. He looked very wise. "Please feel free to ask any and all questions. It is the desire of the emperor to have the world learn of this very sacred place. You have come highly recommended to the emperor, and he is anxious to see your work."

"What are those urns on that shelf?" I asked.

"They are the remains of the Chinese emperors of the past five hundred years," the guide replied.

"They are absolutely beautiful," I said without a pause.

I stood speechless, to say the least, for what seemed an eternity. I glanced around the mine in awe. I turned to the guide and said, "I need to know the history of this amazing place, the history of every emperor and their families, the history of the workers, what every detail means to the Chinese people." I paused to catch my breath.

"That's a large order," the man said in the ruby-red coat replied. "But I will try and give you much knowledge and history of this place."

I stopped, took in a deep breath, hoping the air contained special powers. Hoping that the jade had magical magnetic connections to my body. I could feel the energy swirling around my entire being.

"I want to know the mythology and the legend of this amazing place," I said.

I could practically smell the Pulitzer Prize.

CHAPTER TWO

It was the worse monsoon season that anyone in China under the age of one hundred years had ever seen.

Ag Leh, a six-year-old Chinese girl with blue-black hair and enchanting eyes, ran her fingers through her hair. Her hair was long and hung down to her waist because her parents could not afford scissors to cut it; otherwise, they would have cut it and sold it on the black market.

Money is scarce in the slums. Life is very difficult living in poverty. Family members have to share everything from food to clothing to housing.

Ag Leh, her parents, and grandparents all shared a small eight-by-ten-foot building made out of found pieces of wood, scrap pieces of metal, cardboard, twine, and anything else they could find in dumps or just discarded beside the paths.

There were hundreds of similar structures in this makeshift village. The shacks were almost exact copies of each other. No one would dare place anything of value in view of the other inhabitants for fear it would be stolen.

If you did have anything of monetary or sentimental value, you and your family members would have buried it in the middle of your hut under the cooking pit. The fire continued all day and all night. It was the only source of heat, light, and cooking. The cooking pit was treasured and worshiped.

The monsoon had made everything damp and disgusting. Ag Leh's family dug a trench around their shack to help divert water away, and to this point, the trench had helped.

Ag Leh's mother was squatting over the fire, fixing the meager meal of rice and whatever vegetables she could acquire.

The rains had let up, and Ag Leh was out exploring and trying to find some kids to play with. She never wandered far because her grandparents had scared her with the evils of the outside world.

Ag Leh's father and grandparents entered the shack, and her mother went outside and yelled her name. Ag Leh appeared from the back of the next shack. She ran to her mother and grabbed her hand. They entered the shack, and they all sat down to their evening meal.

The rains started again, so it was time to stay inside and settle into their tarp and blanket beds. They have formed a mound of dirt to get out of the water for each family member. They covered the mound with plastic and then covered the plastic with blankets or anything else to keep the chill at bay. Ag Leh slept in the middle so everyone could protect her from all harm.

Morning arrived, and it was still raining, and the sky was dark, but not as dark as nighttime. Everyone got up, stoked the fire to heat the shack, and prepared rice for breakfast along with tea.

Soon the rained stopped, but the sky was still covered with black billowing clouds. Ag Leh was allowed to go out and see if she could find anyone to play with.

Ag Leh was picking up sticks, thinking she could take them back to her parents for the fire, when she spotted a dog watching her. The pug looked friendly, so she ran over to pet it. The dog stepped back, sniffed her, and then stepped toward her. Ag Leh bent down and pet the little pup on the head. The dog saw the stick and tried to steal it, but Ag Leh held tight. The pup tried again and got the stick from Ag Leh and ran through the maze of shacks, with Ag Leh running as fast as she could, but the dog was always a couple of yards ahead of her.

The dog got to the edge of the community of shacks and turned to make sure his new friend was following him, and the pup started to run up a stone path up the hill. Ag Leh stopped at the last shack and hesitated to follow the pup because she had never been this far from her parents. What if she got lost? Who would know which direction to look in? The dog barked, and Ag Leh forgot about being lost and chased the pup up the hill.

The hill was steep, and the path was windy, so the pug stopped at every curve to make sure that Ag Leh was following him. The dog stopped at an outcropping of rocks, and Ag Leh caught up after a few minutes. Ag Leh grabbed the stick from the pug and said, "There, now I can return home."

At that moment, Ag Leh and the dog heard a roar in the distance. They both looked down into the valley below them and saw a wall of water coming toward the community of shacks. The dam above the shacks was holding back the monsoon's water, but there was too much water for the dam, and the dam broke. The water rushed toward the doomed shacks. The little girl and the dog watched as all the shacks were washed away down stream in an instant.

Ag Leh thought that she heard her mother scream her name, but the sound of the rushing water was the loudest noise she had ever heard.

Within minutes, the valley was washed clean of the shacks and its inhabitants. Ag Leh sat there, stunned. She reached over to the dog and held the dog close to her chest and just hugged him with all her might. She was not old enough to really realize that her life had just changed in an instant, but she was old enough to realize that she would never see her parents or her grandparents ever again.

Ag Leh and her new companion sat on the rock formation for hours. The pug got restless and started to climb higher up the mountain and Ag Leh followed. The pug found berries for Ag Leh to eat and a stream where they both could get a drink of water. Then the pup led her to what looked like a small cave. It was only a rock that stuck out of the mountain, but it was enough of a roof to get them under cover before the rain started again.

The day was ending, and it looked like the rains were going to begin again. The pug snuggled up to Ag Leh, and they fell asleep for the night under the rock. The pair was dry, warm, and Ag Leh's belly full with berries. The sound of the pounding rain put them both to sleep.

CHAPTER THREE

The sun crept under the rock, and the pug opened one eye and then the other. He nuzzled Ag Leh, and she slowly woke up. She reached out to pet the pug. The pug licked her hand, and she smiled.

"I'm going to call you Friend because you have been a very true friend to me," she whispered. "We need to see what is happening out from under this rock."

The monsoon had passed during the night, but the ground was still very wet, and the sun made it look like spirits had dropped diamonds.

Friend took the lead and headed up the hill following the path, and Ag Leh stayed within sight. Ag Leh turned around and saw the valley off in the distance, and there was nothing to see. No shacks, no people, no signs of life that she had been used to.

About two hours of climbing brought the two travelers to the top of the hill. Friend sat down, and Ag Leh plopped right beside him as she was exhausted from the morning climb. Luckily, they sat right next to a patch of berries. Ag Leh picked some and enjoyed getting food into her stomach but wondered if she would find any food for Friend. She found some water and a rock shaped like a bowl, so she brought Friend a bowl of water, and Friend licked feverishly.

Once recovered from hunger, they got to their feet, and they stumbled onto a dirt road. They started walking in the direction of the sunrise.

It wasn't long before they were standing beside a large stone wall with the largest carved wooden doors that Ag Leh had ever seen. Friend found a shady spot under the bush, stamped down a bed of grass, and lay down. Ag Leh stood in front of the door and raised her hand and knocked. There was no sound, and no one answered the door. She sat down beside Friend.

The sun rose higher into the sky, and soon an old man pulling a cart filled with rice appeared. He stopped in front of the double doors and walked up to the door and was about ready to knock when he noticed this little girl with a little pug.

"Who are you?" he asked with a smile.

"I'm Ag Leh, and this is Friend, my best friend," Ag Leh replied.

"Where did you come from?" he questioned why a little girl was out at that hour by herself.

"I came from over that way, and there was lots of water," she said.

He had heard the news of the dam burst and the damage to the shelters and the lives of the residents.

He bowed to her and she returned the gesture. "I am Fang. I am glad to meet you. Were you sent to the orphanage by the authorities?" he asked.

"I have seen no one," she replied.

"Let's see if I can get you and Friend something to eat," he said as he knocked on the door.

"The lady of the house is rather slow answering the door even though I am here every morning for the past sixteen years at the same time," he said, hoping to get a little sympathy.

One of the two doors opened, and there stood a sturdy older woman in worn-out clothes. "Did you get me some rice for the children, Fang?" the woman asked.

"Lee, I have delivered rice here for the past sixteen years, and you always have the same question," Fang replied.

"Who's the girl?" Lee asked, sounding very grumpy.

"I thought you might know. She was sitting here with her dog when I got here," Fang said.

"Little girl, do you need food?" Lee asked.

Ag Leh looked upward with large hungry eyes.

"Come with me, little girl," Lee said while Fang delivered the rice inside the door. "Thank you, Fang," Lee said as he headed to his cart. "He's a very nice man even though he might look a little scary. He wouldn't hurt anyone and would help everyone."

Ag Leh stood up, and Friend jumped up right beside her.

"Come with me," Lee said as she took Ag Leh's hand. They stepped inside the stonewalled orphanage with Friend at their heels.

"No dogs!" Lee said as she slammed the door.

CHAPTER FOUR

The huge doors slammed shut behind Ag Leh and Lee. Lee led the little girl down the long stone-lined hallway.

"The kitchen is in the rear on this floor. The girls' room is there," Lee said as she pointed to the left. "And the boys' room is over there." She pointed to the right. "The main hall is for dining, general gatherings, and for celebrations and is located next to the kitchen," Lee continued as they marched to the kitchen.

"I am the cook, and we need to start breakfast, for the children will be getting up shortly, and I will introduce you to the headmaster after breakfast," Lee said as she shifted the rice bag she was carrying.

They reached the kitchen, which was also made of stones. Scattered everywhere were a large work table, an old oven, a fireplace tall enough to walk into with chimney hooks, soapstone sink that looked large enough to be a bathtub, utensils hanging from ceiling racks, pots and pans covering the walls, and utensils in jars. There was one window that was large enough to light up the entire kitchen. Ag Leh had never seen such a place and so much equipment.

"Take a seat on the table, and stay out of my way," Lee said. "I have my routine." Lee looked like a whirlwind as she glided across the floor. She knew every inch of the kitchen and right where everything was so it was easy for her to prepare the meals for all the children and the headmaster.

Within a few minutes, Ag Leh was taking in new smells, and she watched in amazement as Lee prepared a full meal from almost nothing.

"I have been here for years and can make do with very little," Lee said. "The orphanage does not have a lot of money, so we have to make do with what we have. The children are here because they have no family except the family they make here. It's not the best situation for a child, but it is better than being alone in the woods or living alone on a riverbank. The headmaster tries his best to find homes, but there are few people who want to take a child into their home."

"Give me the salt, please," Lee said not missing a beat. "You may be one of the lucky ones when we get you fed and cleaned up. A good scrubbing will be good for you, and it'll make you feel better inside and out. Now I need pepper."

Ag Leh was more than happy to help Lee because she suddenly felt safe in the kitchen and under the watchful eye of the cook.

"Let's go to the dining room and make sure the kids have the tables set," Lee said as she took Ag Leh's hand and headed through an arched doorway.

Ag Leh looked in awe as they entered the dining hall. Stone walls with great windows of colored glass, large thick wooden dining tables, and tall chairs. Chairs were much too large for children, Ag Leh thought. Lanterns hung from the walls and from big wooden wagon wheels suspended from the ceiling.

There were children younger, older, and of Ag Leh's age busily setting the tables and making sure everything was ready for breakfast.

"Let's get back to the kitchen and get breakfast ready to serve," Lee said, and they walked back through the arched doorway.

Lee got bowls and platters from the cupboards and prepared the food for the tables. Rice, vegetables, a little bit of pork, and tea was the menu for today as well as tomorrow and the next day.

The older children entered the kitchen in a line, and each child carried a bowl or a platter back to the tables. The oldest children were allowed to carry the tea because the pots were very hot.

"Come with me, Ag Leh. We need to find a place to sit and have breakfast too," Lee said. They entered the dining room, and it was now full of children of all ages and sizes. They were all clean, and their clothes might have been used and worn, but they were clean. Ag Leh looked down at her dirty clothes, and she almost started to cry.

"What is wrong?" Lee asked.

"My clothes are dirty and torn," Ag Leh replied.

"We will get you new clothes after breakfast. Don't be upset because every child in this room was in your exact place their first day here. They know what it is like to have nothing and no parents, so they will not make fun of you. They will be willing to become your friends. Trust me, and by tomorrow, you will be feeling much better," Lee said, hoping that her predictions would become truth.

The room was filled with lots of chatter from the children, and then a door creaked, and a large figure entered the room.

The figure moved slowly from the shadows, and Ag Leh thought the figure loomed one hundred times larger than the largest child in the room. She sat there amazed, in awe, and deathly afraid of that man.

"That, Ag Leh, is the headmaster," Lee whispered as the room went dead quiet.

The headmaster took his place at the head table and welcomed all the children and told them that they could now enjoy their meal. The children ate in silence.

"The headmaster likes the children to eat in peace and quiet, and all the children know it, so they all behave. The children who live here know that they have it better than a lot of children even those with families. Here, the headmaster tries to take care of the children and find them homes."

Ag Leh sat beside Lee and enjoyed the warm meal, and then she suddenly thought about Friend outside the stone walls with nothing to eat.

After the meal was finished, the children returned to their chores. Some cleared the tables. Some washed the tables. The older children went into the kitchen and washed the dishes, the pots and pans, and put everything away. By the time Lee and Ag Leh walked through the arched doorway, the kitchen was neat and tidy.

"The headmaster expects everyone to work, and there are more than enough chores for everyone," Lee said as she looked down at Ag Leh.

"You need to meet the headmaster. We need to get you scrubbed up and get some other clothes. Please come with me, and let's see what we can do," Lee said as she led the way to the girls' room.

Lee showed Ag Leh where she could get cleaned up and told her that she would get her some newer clothes. "But first I have something I have to do, and I will be right back," Lee said as she left the room.

Chapter Five

The "no dog" rule was not Lee's rule but the rule from the headmaster of the orphanage.

Lee opened the double doors and presented Friend with a bowl of rice, vegetables, and pork, food she saved from breakfast.

Friend's eyes lit up, and he licked Lee's hand.

"The 'no dog' rule is not my rule. I will find you food somewhere," Lee said as she stepped back into the stonewalled orphanage.

Friend ate the rice mixture, then laid in the nest he had made, stomach full and ready for a morning nap.

CHAPTER SIX

Lee returned to the girls' room where Ag Leh was waiting for her. Ag Leh felt alone even though the room had four long rows of beds. Each girl was given a bed, coverings, and a small trunk for her belongings. Everyone had to keep their bed area clean, and they all had to help clean the common areas. Ag Leh patiently waited for Lee and didn't try to speak to anyone.

"You can talk to the other kids, you know," Lee said to Ag Leh as she approached her.

"I know, but I don't know anyone, and I was afraid they would make fun of me," Ag Leh said.

"Here, I found a dress that I thought would fit you. I hope you like it," Lee said as she handed her a simple grey cotton dress.

"Thank you. This is the nicest dress I have ever had," Ag Leh said as she accepted the dress.

"We need to introduce you to the headmaster. I told him about you, and he needs to meet you in order to decide if you can stay or find some other place to send you," Lee said.

Ag Leh looked puzzled. She thought that she had found a home, but now she may be put outside of the safety of the orphanage. Lee had made her feel welcome, but that could change in an instant. What if the headmaster thought that she was a trouble-maker or a brat or a thief? What if he just didn't like the way she looked? What if he was in a bad mood?

"Don't worry, dear child. I am going to tell him that you helped me in the kitchen this morning without me even asking and that I could use a good pair of hands morning, noon, and night."

This gave Ag Leh a little hope of staying, and the knot in her stomach settled a little, but the knot was still there.

Lee and Ag Leh got organized and walked out into the hall, through the kitchen, and back through the dining room. They walked toward the door that the headmaster entered the dining room from. Ag Leh was still a little scared but tried not to show it.

Lee knocked on the door, and the deep voice inside said to enter. Ag Leh grabbed Lee's hand and squeezed it hard. Would she be out in the street in a couple of minutes or working in the kitchen with Lee?

They entered the headmaster's office, and Ag Leh saw him sitting behind his wooden desk. The only items on the desk were yellowed paper, sealing wax, and a pen. The headmaster wore a signet ring to seal his letters.

"Good morning, Ag Leh," the headmaster said. "Lee told me a little about your ordeal, and I am very sorry for your loss. This is an orphanage for parentless children, and we believe you lost your parents. You probably lost all your personal papers too. Have you found this place to suit you? We would like our children to want to be here and contribute to the operation by helping each other."

"This is a very nice place, and Lee has been very kind to me," Ag Leh said.

"Headmaster, Ag Leh was very helpful to me this morning, and I could use her hands in the kitchen to help prepare the meal. I think she would be very useful, and I would hope we could find a bed for her and let her stay," Lee spoke in a direct tone so the headmaster would know that she was sincere.

"On your recommendation, Lee, I will let her stay and help you, so you will directly supervise her. If she needs anything out of the normal items, please let me," the headmaster said. "You may go now and get her a bed and get her settled in."

"Thank you," Lee said.

"Thank you," Ag Leh echoed. The two turned around and left the room.

When they had closed the door behind them, Ag Leh thanked Lee.

"We need to get you a bed, introduce you to some of the other children and then start the mid-day meal," Lee said.

A sense of peace passed through Ag Leh, and the knot in her stomach was suddenly gone. "What about Friend?"

"I gave her some food after breakfast," Lee said.

"I think she is a boy dog. Can I go with you next time?" Ag Leh asked.

"Of course you can," Lee replied.

They didn't say another word until they reached the kitchen.

CHAPTER SEVEN

Ag Leh was given a bed between two girls of different ages. The girls are placed next to someone older and someone younger. The girls help each other to learn new words, learn new skills, and with reading and math. The older ones helped the younger children.

Ag Leh had never been to school, so she was behind most of the children in education except for the very young.

Meilin, who was older than Ag Leh, immediately realized that Ag Leh had never had any formal education and was very kind to her and helped her with her new daily duties.

Meilin taught her the proper way to make her bed, organize her trunk, and tidy up her area. Ag Leh was very appreciative of Meilin efforts.

Jun, who had the bed on the other side of Ag Leh, was younger and needed help doing her duties because of a recent accident that dislocated her shoulder.

Once Ag Leh learned the proper way of making the bed, she helped Jun make her bed and other duties.

The large, long room was filled with girls ranging in age from four to sixteen. By the age of sixteen the girls, if not adopted, were found a job and inexpensive housing. But while they were at the orphanage, they were given the opportunity to increase their education and skills, skills that would aid them in taking care of a home. These lessons learned in this living experience would also help them to form relationships with these children and with adults later in life.

Every week, the girls were given different duties to perform. This week, it was Ag Leh's turn to sweep all the floors. This included the floors in the girls' room, the boys' room, the dining hall, and of course the kitchen.

An old woman who mysteriously appeared once a week cleaned the headmaster's residence. Ag Leh thought that the headmaster must have hired her out of mercy to her. She was very old, couldn't move very fast, and was bowed over with curved bones. Ag Leh felt sorry for her, but the woman always had a smile on her face and a warm greeting for each of the children.

Ag Leh was amazed of how this woman, who was there only once a week, knew each child by name.

CHAPTER EIGHT

Ag Leh enjoyed all the girls, but she especially liked having Meilin and Jun as her closest room-mates. Meilin would share her love of books as well as her books. Meilin taught her that books could teach her very valuable lessons and also take her to foreign places that she would never be able to go to on her own. Reading opened up Meilin and Ag Leh's imagination. The imagination they both will use their entire life.

CHAPTER NINE

Every morning, Ag Leh would wake up before the other children and go to the kitchen to see Lee. Lee would now give Ag Leh a bowl of yesterday's evening meal so she could feed Friend.

Ag Leh would pet him on the head and give him the bowl of food. Friend would sometime roll over and have Ag Leh rub his belly, which always made Ag Leh laugh out loud.

Ag Leh was so happy that Friend had stayed near her and had not wandered off. She hoped that someday Friend would be allowed to live with her and her new family.

This particular morning, there were two figures walking up the dirt road. As they approached, Ag Leh could see that one was dressed in a gold coat and the other in a matching silver coat. They looked very distinguished, but for some reason, she was a little suspicious of them because she had never seen them before nor anyone that dressed like them.

"Good morning, child," they both said in unison. "Today is very pleasant, and what a beautiful little dog you have. It is nice to have a companion for you to play with."

"Good morning. My dog's name is Friend, and he has helped me a lot," Ag Leh replied.

"Do you live at the orphanage?" the person in gold asked.

"Yes," Ag Leh replied. "They are very nice to me here."

The two people bowed and then turned away and continued their walk.

"I wonder who they are," Ag Leh said to herself, and then she continued to rub Friend's belly.

Ag Leh forgot about the time because of the strangers that passed by. She jumped up from the ground and ran into the orphanage and shut the doors behind her. She ran to the kitchen, and Lee just smiled at her. Lee knew that the precious few seconds that Ag Leh spends with Friend were Ag Leh's escape from the orphanage and always brightened her morning.

"Let's get to work. We have a lot of hungry bellies to fill," Lee said with a smile, knowing that Ag Leh was the best helper she could have prayed for.

"You look a little a puzzled this morning," Lee said.

"While I was playing with Friend, a couple of people stopped and talked to me," Ag Leh said. "They were pleasant enough and dressed identical except for the color of their coats. I had never seen them before, and they surprised me."

"I am sure they are fine people," Lee replied. "And I hope you greeted them kindly."

"I did," Ag Leh said, and then she got busy sorting through the rice.

CHAPTER TEN

Ag Leh found that she had a particular talent that all the girls loved. Ag Leh started by braiding Jun's hair, and then Meilin wanted her hair braided. Soon all the girls wanted their hair braided, and Ag Leh became very excited to have so many news friends.

Ag Leh started by braiding three strands of hair together and then braiding braids together to form designs. She then tried to braid four and then five strands of hair together, and soon she was creating works of art on the girls' heads.

Lee asked her where she discovered this ability, and Ag Leh replied, "There was a woman in our village that would braid string together and then ropes to make them stronger, and then one day I saw that she had braided this girl's hair. I thought that the girl's hair was beautiful and wanted to try braiding their hair. The woman taught me to braid ropes, but I had never tried anyone's hair until I got here."

"You make the girls very happy when you braid their hair," Lee said. "Maybe someday you could braid mine."

Lee had a very long hair, and after breakfast Ag Leh asked Lee if she wanted her hair braided, and Lee agreed.

Ag Leh braided Lee hair into one large braid and then wrapped that braid around Lee's head and secured it with a pin.

"Thank you," Lee said. "That is beautiful work, and it gets my hair out of my work."

"You are welcome," Ag Leh replied. "And you look wonderful too."

Ag Leh would braid anything she could find. She was soon braiding tiebacks for all the curtain, cords to hang kitchen items, and trims that became decorations on pillows. The headmaster even noticed Ag Leh's talent and asked her to braid him a belt out of some excess leather he had when he had shoes made.

Ag Leh felt that she had finally become part of the orphanage family, and that made her feel good inside.

CHAPTER ELEVEN

Ag Leh was in the kitchen with Lee cleaning up after the noontime meals when word was sent from the headmaster's office for Ag Leh to join him.

Ag Leh walked through the dining room toward the headmaster's door, and the door opened before she could knock.

Inside the headmaster's office stood the couple that Ag Leh had spoken to many days before, and they were still wearing matching coat but in different colors.

"Good afternoon, Ag Leh," the headmaster said as she approached his desk. "I want to introduce you to Yin Yin and Yang Yang."

"Good afternoon," Ag Leh said as she looked in shock because she had met them on the road in the early morning hours.

Yin Yin and Yang Yang bowed toward Ag Leh, and Ag Leh bowed too.

"They have come to adopt a child and raise that child as their own," the headmaster said. "They noticed all of the braiding that had been done of the girls' hair and wanted to meet the person that braided their hair."

"We were impressed with your braiding ability and technique and wanted to meet you," Yin Yin said.

"You do very fine and meticulous work," Yang Yang chimed in.

"They own a business that makes household knives and thought that you might be able to braid the handles for them," the headmaster said.

"We make very fine items and want to make them more beautiful with hand-braided handles," Yang Yang said.

"They would like to take you to their home and raise you as their daughter," the headmaster said as he nodded to the two dressed in silk embroidered coat.

"We would very much like to make you part of our family," Yin Yin said. "We will teach you many trades, which will be invaluable to you and your future."

Ag Leh was caught totally by surprised. She was sure that every child in the orphanage had wished for such a gift as becoming a family, but she just didn't like the looks of this couple.

"Ag Leh, I would like you to acquire your belongings and prepare to leave with this very distinguished couple," the headmaster said. "They will leave within the hour."

Ag Leh bowed to the headmaster and to the couple and left the room.

"We will take care of the financial part of the matter within the hour," the headmaster said.

"We will gladly pay for this girl," Yang Yang said. "She will be a very valuable asset to us. We will surely make our money back."

"Please make yourselves comfortable in our dining room while Ag Leh gets her things," the headmaster said as he led them to the door.

The headmaster started to close the door; he watched the couple walk over to a couple of chairs. He wondered what they had meant by making their money back. He wondered if he had made a mistake and had now changed Ag Leh's destiny. Maybe he could have gotten even more money out of them, he thought.

CHAPTER TWELVE

Ag Leh ran to the kitchen to tell Lee about the predicament. She told her that the couple whom she had seen weeks before while she was playing with Friend was adopting her. She also told Lee that she was scared to go with them.

"Ag Leh, they are probably very fine people, and you are lucky to have someone want to adopt you," Lee said. "Every child wished that they would be adopted, but you are the one who is being adopted. You have a chance to have a family and, sometime in the future, have a family of your own."

Ag Leh understood every word Lee had spoken, but she was still scared.

CHAPTER THIRTEEN

Ag Leh met the couple, the headmaster, and Lee in the dining room carrying the few meager items that she had acquired.

"Ag Leh, I will really miss your help in the kitchen," Lee said with a tear starting to appear in her eye. She knew that she would probably never see Ag Leh again.

"I wish you all the happiness in the world," the headmaster said. "I am sure you will be very happy with your new family.

"We are very pleased to call you our family," Yin Yin said.

"I hope that the payment is sufficient?" Yang Yang said to the headmaster as a thick envelope was handed to the headmaster.

"I am sure this will take care of everything," the headmaster said, and in return he handed the couple a very thin envelope holding Ag Leh's papers.

Because she had lost everything in the flood, the headmaster had new papers prepared. They may not be entirely correct, but who would care about the papers of a girl from an orphanage who parents were killed in a flood.

Everyone bowed to each other, and Yin Yin took Ag Leh's hand and guided her to the hallway and toward the double doors. Yang Yang followed close behind. The headmaster returned to his secluded quarters to count his money.

Lee shuffled to the kitchen to prepare for the evening meal. Her thoughts were for Ag Leh's happiness, but she too had disturbing feelings about this couple. She didn't know why she felt that way, but it was her instinct taking hold. She knew there was something bad that would come out in the future and that the headmaster had made a terrible mistake.

But this was not the first misdeed that the headmaster had ever made. Money had always played a more valuable role in his life than the welfare of the children.

Chapter Fourteen

As Ag Leh and her new parents prepared to leave the orphanage, and as they reached the double doors, Ag Leh asked them for a favor.

"Can I take my dog, Friend, with me?" Ag Leh asked, not sure of the response.

"We usually don't have animals around, but I will make an exception this time," Yin Yin said. "You will need to take care of your dog's needs, and we will provide the food. I think your dog will help in your transition into our family."

Ag Leh picked him up into her arms. Ag Leh felt safe with Friend, and now they were on another one of life's adventures, even though she had some uneasiness about the situation.

CHAPTER FIFTEEN

Ag Leh was very impressed by Yin Yin and Yang Yang's home.

It was a very nice house with beautiful yards. Much time had to be spent in taking care of the yards and gardens, but they hired people to do that.

They had a secured vegetable garden that only they had access to. They were very suspicious of others touching their food.

Inside the house was beautiful furnishings that looked like they had been passed down through many generations.

The table was set for the evening meal with expensive glassware, china, and flatware. Maybe Ag Leh was luckier than she had thought. Maybe they were wonderful people. Maybe her physical feelings of dread were brought on by irrational thoughts.

They showed her the house and then the bedroom that she would be sharing with Friend.

She stood there in amazement that she would have her own room. This room was about fives times larger than the shack that she shared with her parents and grandparents. She didn't realize that children could have such surroundings.

"We hope you like your room, Ag Leh," Yin Yin said. "We have extra blankets and pillows in the closet if you need them. We want you to be very comfortable here. This is now your home."

"We prepare our own food here and would like you to help us," Yang Yang said. "We prefer to prepare our own food because sometimes the help will try to poison people of wealth to take their belongings, so we do not hire anyone to work within the house. We only hire people to work on the grounds. They are not allowed in the house."

Ag Leh tried to understand, but she never had anything worth stealing, so she didn't actually understand the reason. But she enjoyed being in the kitchen helping anyway.

They walked to the kitchen. It was larger than the kitchen at the orphanage. The shelves were stocked with rows of jars containing spices and herbs. There were shelves lined with jars of preserved meats and vegetables. There were rows of dishes, serving vessels, utensils, cooking items, and anything any cook could imagine.

"We are going to make a meal of pork, vegetables, and rice," Yin Yin said.

The meal sounded very similar to what Lee made at the orphanage. But when it was prepared and served, it did not even look like the food Lee had prepared for the many mouths of the orphanage. This meal was far superior to Lee's cooking, but Yin Yin and Yang Yang were only cooking for three people, and their ingredients were fresher and more abundant.

"Thank you for dinner," Ag Leh said at the end of the meal. "That was the best meal of my life. And thank you for feeding Friend in the kitchen."

"It is our pleasure. You are now part of our family, and we want the best for you," Yin Yin said. "We want you to be happy with us and with your home, and that means Friend is also part of our family."

"Tomorrow we still start your training in our business," Yang Yang said. "There is much to learn, and many secrets you will learn. Now you need to sleep. Enjoy your new bed and room."

Ag Leh left the table and went to her room, with Friend following her. She had never slept alone except for her evening with Friend, and once again, it will be a night with only Friend by her side.

CHAPTER SIXTEEN

The next morning, Ag Leh and Friend awoke to the smells coming from the kitchen.

They went to the kitchen, and they were greeted with a "good morning" from Yin Yin.

Yang Yang was preparing the table while Yin Yin cooked the meal of rice, eggs, preserved meat, and marinated fruit.

"This smells very good," Ag Leh said.

Friend noticed his portion in a bowl on the floor. He went to the bowl and ate all that was in the bowl.

"We have never had a pug in the house before, and it is entertaining. Maybe he will be a good watchdog and tell us when someone is around," Yin Yin said. "We can always use more security."

"I think he will let us know when people are around," Ag Leh said. "He seems curious, and he also wants to protect me."

"Here, sit right down. This is your seat at the table. Enjoy your breakfast," Yang Yang said. "Soon we will take you to our workshop where we make household knives. It is an art that has been passed down through seven generations in my family," Yang Yang continued. "I am very proud to be a katana maker—I mean, knife maker."

That was one of the secrets. They were not just common household knife makers; they were katana makers. For generations, Yang Yang's family had made swords for the killing of dragons. Dragon hearts and horns have mystical and magical powers that the war barons of China wanted to acquire, and the only way to get those powers was to kill the dragon, chop off its horns, and cut out its heart.

Little did Ag Leh realize what the headmaster had gotten her into because she had no idea what the word *katana* meant.

CHAPTER SEVENTEEN

Yin Yin and Yang Yang let Ag Leh enjoy her new home for a couple of days to gain her trust. They fed her and Friend well and made sure they had time for play and lots of time to rest throughout the day.

Each evening, they all helped to prepare the evening meal and then it was time for Ag Leh to get her sleep.

On the fifth day, they decided that it was time to indoctrinate Ag Leh into the family business.

After breakfast, they escorted her to a workshop at the rear of their estate. "This," Yang Yang began, "is where we forge the iron to make the knives, swords, and other weaponry that we are famous for. We find the best iron sand and coal in the world, and we turn that into steel, and then that is sent to the sword smiths who work their magic, and then it is finally sent to the polisher and finishers to finalize the sword. You, young lady, will work on the handle covering. We want to produce the most beautiful braided handles the world has ever seen."

"With your young eyes, your sensitive touch, and your sense of style, we are positive we can produce the handles the world desires. You will become an intricate part of the family business and make us famous."

"Let me show you your workspace," Yin Yin said. "We have a corner all set up for you. We have many pieces of the finest leather in many beautiful colors. There are sharp knives for cutting and all the tools any leather smith would be proud to own. If there is any tool you may ever need, you only need to tell us, and we will provide it."

Ag Leh stood in disbelief. She was not brought here to be their only child; she was brought here to be their only child laborer. She felt like she was going to be imprisoned for the rest of her life performing work for their greed and aspirations.

But Ag Leh bowed and smiled because she knew she needed to gain their trust and allegiance.

"We will begin making the katana swords next week. The work takes a long time, and you will be at the end of the process," Yin Yin said. "But you can practice your skills now. You can design the handle coverings and figure out the supplies you will need."

"We would also like to train you in martial arts so you will appreciate the instruments that you will be working on. The more you know about weight, balance, and force, the more you will appreciate our art form," Yang Yang said. "We make the best katana swords that are the most requested in all of Asia. Stay here and get used to your area, and we will get you before lunch."

Yin Yin and Yang Yang turned and walked away. They knew that Ag Leh could not escape because their compound was secure. The only way in or out is through a door that is locked at all times. The gardeners have to be escorted in; they were being watched all the time they are working, and then they are escorted out. Security is of the upmost importance to Yin Yin and Yang Yang, and soon, Ag Leh would find out why.

Chapter Eighteen

Martial arts training began that very afternoon. They brought in a martial arts instructor to show Ag Leh the basics. He explained the physical, the emotional, and the spiritual aspects of this ancient form of warfare.

"We will begin with learning how to breathe and relax," the instructor said. "You must be able to relax in order to totally concentrate on what you are doing. You must breathe deep in order to get the oxygen to your body and get the energy flowing within yourself."

The instructor took a deep breath, and Ag Leh copied him. She copied every movement that he made, and he watched her carefully and would correct her as they proceeded.

"You are a good student," the instructor said. "You will learn quickly and become a great warrior."

At the end of the first lesson, they both bowed. "You will be a good student," the instructor reassured her. "We will continue your lessons next week.

The instructor went to the main part of the house, and he was escorted out of the walled estate. Yin Yin paid the instructor and set up the time for the next class.

The martial arts instructor was no more trustworthy in the eyes of Yin Yin and Yang Yang than any other person they employed.

CHAPTER NINETEEN

During the following weeks, there was a fury of activity on the grounds. Men started delivering iron sand and coal by the cartloads into the workshop at the rear of the property. The pile of iron sand grew until it was meters over Ag Leh's head.

They built a special kiln to produce the high heat needed to manipulate the iron sand into the steel that would be used for the swords.

The basement of the house was where the finishing work took place so that Yin Yin and Yang Yang could keep watch on all the work and to make sure nothing was stolen. Supplies were delivered to the basement as well.

Then the day came when the smelting processing began. They built the clay vessel that would house the fire that would melt the iron sand and coal into the world's finest steel. The fire was started, and it was a long time before it reached the desired temperature.

The work was hard, and the temperature was very hot. The men grew tired working day and night to keep an eye on this most valuable steel.

The men watched the fire and added the iron sand and coal to the fire and waited and watched for four days.

On the fourth day, they destroyed the vessel and pulled out the steel boom. The sword smiths chose the best core steel and the best skin steel for the beginning process of making the katana.

Now the forging process begins. The core steel had to be hammered and folded and hammered again. Repeating the process made the strongest steel and removed impurities.

The skin steel had to be repeatedly folded and hammered to build up its strength and remove the impurities of the iron. The most pure and strongest steel was needed for the katana.

The work was hard, and the days were long, and the finished steel looked indestructible.

Then the men had to shape the skin of the blade, and then they would hammer the core of the blade into the skin cover.

The blade then had clay painstakingly painted onto the blade in different thicknesses before quenching the blade into water. The thin layer over the razor-sharp edge would produce stronger steel that can hold an edge. Thicker layers of clay on the back of the blade made softer steel that was more resilient. The backside of the blade was used for defense, and the sharp edge was used for killing.

The work in the shed was completed, and the blades were carried over to the main house where the finishing work would begin.

CHAPTER TWENTY

Ag Leh was encouraged to watch the old men at work. Ag Leh withstood the heat and watched long hours as the men constantly added iron sand and coal to the vessel. They sweat from the intense heat; the color of their skin turned a bright red as they approached the vessel and then returned to a dark tan when they stepped away.

Ag Leh had no knowledge of steel making, and someday it was hoped that she would become an expert and a highly demanded specialist in China.

When the vessel was smashed, Ag Leh couldn't believe her eyes. The sight of the intense heat filling the work area, the intense color of the coal and steel, the cracking sounds hurting her ears, and the exhausted dedicated men tending to their duties.

They pulled the steel bloom out of the fire, and the steel bloom was too hot to handle, too precious not to be drawn in by its searing beauty, too dangerous to get too close to. Ag Leh stayed her distance.

CHAPTER TWENTY-ONE

The workmen left as fast as they arrived. The steel bloom had been made. The core steel had been imbedded into the skin steel covering, the forging was completed, and the quenching was done. The hardened steel swords were delivered to the basement of the main house where the polishing and finishing processes would take place. Where Ag Leh's artistry would have a chance to shine.

Yin Yin and Yang Yang took Ag Leh to the basement.

"We will be polishing and finishing the swords," Yin Yin said. "We have had many years of experience and have perfected our trades. We will help you to learn the entire process. Your young eyes will see things that we can no longer see so we can make the best blades ever made in China. Your sensitive fingers will feel any intrusions, which will need to be addressed. You are part of a team, the world's best katana team in the all of China."

"Why do you make swords?" Ag Leh asked.

"I am going to tell you something that is very important that very few people know," Yang Yang said. "We are dragon hunters, and we need the very best weapons we can find. We find that we can make the most remarkable swords ourselves. Our swords are the best in China. No one makes them better. To slay a dragon, we need the best steel to make the best blades.

"There is a young dragon whose parents and grandparents guard the most valuable jade mine in China. The parents and grandparents are much too large for any human to kill. Only a god could take down such a creature, but our chances are greatly increased if we decide to kill the younger dragon.

"The dragon's horn and heart will give us power that no one has ever seen. We will be able to sell the remaining parts to herbalists throughout the eastern countries. We will be powerful and rich."

Yin Yin walked over to a wall cabinet and pulled out a rolled up paper. He unrolled the paper, and there was a painting of a dragon. The dragon depicted was a magnificent creature with green scales, horns, brilliant black eyes, and breathing fire.

"This is a painting of the young dragon," Yin Yin said. "This dragon will one day be ours. It is known that this dragon's right eye has a blind spot, and this diagram show where he cannot see. So we need to approach the dragon from this angle," Yin Yin pointed to a triangular area. "He will not be able to see us approaching, and we will be able to slice his neck with the katana. One swipe and the dragon's horn and heart will be ours. Our power, our riches, our fame. You will inherit all our money. All of this," Yin Yin gestured with his arms, "will one day be yours."

Ag Leh was in shock. They wanted her to help build a sword to be the instrument to kill a dragon for their own greed. But what could she do? She had no family to return to; she was pretty sure that Yin Yin and Yang Yang had probably given the headmaster a hefty amount of money for her, and he would not take her back because he would not want to return his ill-gotten gain. She hoped that the headmaster didn't do this to other undeserving children. She now considered herself a prisoner, a slave.

CHAPTER TWENTY-TWO

Ag Leh examined the drawing of the dragon, imagining what the skin felt like, the smell of its breath, the heat from its flame, and what it would be like to look directly into its eyes.

Yin Yin left the room, and Yang Yang said, "We have a surprise for you. Such beautiful item that people can only dream of owning."

Yin Yin returned to the room carrying a bolt of red cloth. He unfurled the garment. It was a robe similar to the ones worn by Yin Yin and Yang Yang, except this one was a beautiful ruby red.

The robe was decorated with jewel tones of sapphire blue, amethyst, emerald green, garnet, citrine, and other magnificent colors. There were gold and silver threads that created elaborate designs. On the back was an embroidered dragon with a dagger plunged into its heart. The embossed buttons had the same dragon design. It was the most beautiful garment Ag Leh had ever seen and touched, but it also disturbed her because of the wounded animal on the back.

"This is an exquisite robe that we had made especially for you. It took many hours of handwork to make such a beautiful gown," Yang Yang said. "But we have another great gift for you."

Yang Yang went to the wall, reached up, and took down a katana sword from its resting spot. "This katana sword is yours," Yang Yang said. "But it is not complete. You have the privilege of braiding the handle and personalizing it to your liking. We hope that you enjoy these gifts. Wear them and use them in good health."

"Your martial arts instructor told us what a great student you have become. He said that you are now ready to use a real weapon in class, so we wanted to give you that sword. We wanted you to also dress as the dragon slayer that you will become," Yin Yin said.

"Thank you. The gifts are beautiful," Ag Leh said. "I will take great pride in owning them and will cherish them forever."

Ag Leh draped the robe over her arm and took the sword by the unfinished handle and walked to her workspace.

She hung the robe on a hook on the wall and placed the sword on her workbench. She thought a long time about the design for the handle; then she started slicing thin lengths of leather in several colors including red.

Within a few days, Ag Leh braided an intricate design for her katana, and she made it fit the palm of her hand perfectly. When it was finally done, she picked it up, and it felt as if it was an extension of her arm. She looked down, and it read AG LEH—DRAGON SLAYER.

CHAPTER TWENTY-THREE

Ag Leh spent many nights not sleeping. The only creature that sincerely cared for her was Friend. She would pick up the little pug and hug him so tight. Friend would sleep next to her when she couldn't sleep. He wanted to protect her and keep her safe.

Ag Leh realized that the only way she could survive is to go along with their scheme. She needed to pretend that she enjoyed the martial arts training, the skill of polishing and finishing the blade, the braiding the handles, and being their only child.

But what if they discovered that she didn't like the idea of killing a dragon for their own power and greed? What would they do to her? She needed to make them think that she too wanted to kill that young dragon for her own fortune. She had to prove to them that she was worthy of their loyalty.

She needed to have a family. Her natural family was gone, but they were not greedy nor power hungry; they were just hungry and poor.

Chapter Twenty-Four

Ag Leh introduced multiple colors and started braiding designs into the handles. Yin Yin and Yang Yang were very pleased with the results.

Yin Yin spent his days polishing the blades and making them shine. Yang Yang did the finishing of the blades, making them very sharp, and then worked on the tip of the blade.

They produced only a couple of swords a year, but that was enough to pay their expenses and live comfortably.

Years have past, and Ag Leh was now ten years old. She continued the martial arts classes, and the instructor was very impressed with her concentration and her abilities. Her reputation for braiding the katana handles was known throughout China. People had placed orders years in advance.

The family of three seemed to become a real family. They lived together and worked every day in the workshop and also in the house. Ag Leh did her daily chores and much more. She was a great worker with goals, energy, and ambition.

The day finally came for Yin Yin to tell Ag Leh their next goal for her.

"We need to talk," Yin Yin said to Ag Leh, "about your future and what we see as your future. Yang Yang and I want you to join us as a dragon slayer. It is very honorable position in this land to be a dragon slayer. Remember I showed you the chart depicting the dragon with the blind spot?"

Ag Leh nodded.

"Now it is time for you to be trained as a dragon slayer. There are skills you will need to learn, and there are also tests to prove that you are capable of slaying the dragon," Yin Yin said.

"I don't know if I have the ability to slay a beast such as a dragon," Ag Leh replied. "I don't know if I am capable of killing any creature full of life and mystery."

"You will soon be trained in the art of dragon slaying," Yin Yin said. "And you will also learn about the treasures that you will give the world upon its death."

Yin Yin left the room, giving Ag Leh time to gather her thoughts about becoming a dragon slayer.

CHAPTER TWENTY-FIVE

Ag Leh had trainers and instructors daily for months, teaching her the skills of dragon slaying.

She had to learn the history of the dragons in China. She had to learn about the dragon's abilities and about its physical being. She had to learn about its skin, its scales, and its methane bladder that produced the flames, its flying ability, and other powers it possessed.

Her martial arts teacher taught her the skills to become a dragon slayer.

She had emotional training so that she would be able to kill the beast and not have regrets.

Ag Leh took all the training, and everyone was very pleased with her abilities and enthusiasm.

Ag Leh worked hard, but she pretended that she wanted to become a dragon slayer. She gave them the answers they wanted even though she was lying to herself. She did not want to take the life of a mystical beast. A beast that may never live again.

CHAPTER TWENTY-SIX

"Be aware of your location and surroundings when preparing to slay a dragon," Ag Leh's martial arts instructor said with authority.

"Know who the other dragon slayers are because you must act as one. Keep the sun warming your back. The warmth will sooth your muscles and calm your nerves. The sunlight will also blind the dragon."

Ag Leh nodded and acknowledged that she would always remember everything that she had been taught and use it to the best of her ability.

CHAPTER TWENTY-SEVEN

The day of the final test finally arrived. It had been several years since Yin Yin and Yang Yang adopted Ag Leh. She felt that they were a family, but they had different desires for her future.

Her parents wanted her to become a world-renowned dragon slayer. She was happy working on the katana swords, but she never wanted to use one.

"Today you are going to be tested for your skills and abilities," Yin Yin said. "You look enchanting in your red robe carrying your katana sword. I am sure you will be successful today and then move on to the next level of your career."

"We have created three straw figures for you to practice on," Yang Yang said. "We will take you into the room where they are standing in a row. It is your job to use your sword and remove their head, slice off an arm, and then push your sword into the area of the liver."

Ag Leh nodded, and they walked into the room where there were three straw stick figures standing in a straight row. They had no resemblance to a human, so she had no hesitation to show her parents the skills that she had learned in her martial arts classes.

"You can proceed when you are ready," Yin Yin said.

Ag Leh stood still for a moment and took two deep breaths. She tried to remember everything her instructor had told her and showed her. Then she raised the sword over her head. She swung the sword toward the straw neck, and the head popped off with a perfect slice. She brought the blade back in an upward motion, then removed one arm with a single swipe. She then plunged the tip of the blade into its abdomen and out the other side.

Yin Yin and Yang Yang stood in amazement as they saw their child complete the first part of the first test with ease.

Ag Leh once again took a couple of deep breaths and thought about her training and then proceeded to attack the second straw statue with more energy and more vigor. This time, she performed an upswing to the neck, and the head went flying toward the ceiling, the second blow downward removed its arm, and the final stab into the abdomen was successful.

Once again her parents stood in awe.

Ag Leh approached the third straw man and showed her prowess as she destroyed the third character with more power than she had destroyed the first two.

She bowed toward the straw figures and returned her sword into its sheath. She turned around to look at her parents.

"You have passed your first test of ability and coordination. We are very pleased," Yin Yin said. "You have taken your classes seriously and learned well. We are very pleased with your abilities. Now on to the second test."

Ag Leh figured that the second part of the test would have to be an oral exam to make sure she understood the spiritual and emotional training of martial arts plus confidence, focus, and discipline.

"You must now prove that you can truly become a dragon slayer," Yang Yang said. "We must go to the shed at the back of the yard where your test is waiting."

Chapter Twenty-Eight

Ag Leh, Yin Yin, and Yang Yang walked to the workshop at the back of the estate and entered through the old wooden door. The workshop was divided into several different areas, depending on which part of the swords was being worked on. There were also a couple of small rooms used for storage.

They stood in the middle of the workshop. Yin Yin said, "Behind that door is your final test. If you pass this test, you will become a dragon slayer. If you fail this test, we must decide your future."

Ag Leh looked puzzled and frightened. She thought that it was going to be a test about the spirituality of martial arts, and now she was confused. *What is behind that door? It is too small of a room to contain a real dragon*, she thought.

Ying Ying opened the door, and in the dimly lit room was a mother cat and five kittens enjoying their meal. The mother cat was licking her litter of kittens as they ate. The mother cat looked very content, and the kittens were all struggling with each other to get close to their mother.

"You must take your katana sword and kill the mother cat and then the kittens," Yin Yin said firmly and directly. "This will prove that you have the nerve to take the life of a dragon."

Ag Leh was in shock. She stood there looking at the happy mother cat and the kittens and could not imagine taking their lives away from them.

"Remember, if you fail, we will have to decide your future," Yang Yang said firmly. "At this moment, you are deciding *your* future."

"I can't kill the innocent cat and the kittens," Ag Leh replied.

"If you fail to take their lives," Yang Yang said, "your future will be changed forever. What your destiny *was* is not what it *will be*."

Ag Leh walked into the dimly lit room, and Yang Yang closed the door.

Ag Leh stood in her ruby-red robe with the embroidered dragon on her back. She looked down at the sheath hanging off her shoulder and withdrew the katana sword. She thought of the history of the katana sword. She thought about all her martial arts training. Her hand and arm started shaking. She had never killed anything in her life. How could she kill this innocent cat and new-born kittens?

"What am I going to do?" she said to herself out loud. "If I don't do as I am told, that shows that I do not respect Yin Yin and Yang Yang. If I do what I feel is right in my heart, it will also show that I do not respect them. If I do what they have told me to do, then I do not respect myself."

Ag Leh placed the sword back into the sheath.

The mother cat and her litter lay on a wooden table that was covered with hatchet marks, blood, and oil stains from years gone by. She wondered what had happened in this very room over those many years. Was this the room where young dragon slayers all took their last test? How many passed and how many were true to their hearts?

Ag Leh picked up one of the kittens and placed it on the stone wall while the mother cat watched her every move. Then she picked up the second and third kittens. The mother cat got concerned and scampered over to the kittens. The mother cat picked the kittens up one by one by the nape and put them in a hole in the stone wall. Ag Leh retrieved the last two kittens and placed them where the other three were, and the mother moved them into the hole, and the mother stayed in the wall with the litter.

Ag Leh then walked over to the table, looked down at the dragon buttons on her robe, and withdrew the katana sword from the sheath. She raised it over her head, and with a quick and strong thrust, she slashed the table as hard as she could, and it made a loud cracking sound that filled the little room.

The wooden door swung open.

"What have you done, Ag Leh!" Yang Yang yelled violently. "Where are the cat and the kittens? You have just sealed your fate."

CHAPTER TWENTY-NINE

Nothing more was said within the confines of the dimly lit room in the work shed.

The hours of the afternoon seemed like days to Ag Leh as she and Friend sat in her room.

"Friend, I don't know what is going to happen to me and to you. I am scared. I have studied hard, I have learned how to braid the sword handles, and I have trained hard in my martial arts. All of this shows that I respect them, but by not performing the last dragon slayer test, I have shown them that I do not respect them. But my heart would not let me take the lives of the mother cat and her kittens. What is going to happen to us? I wish I knew. I wish I knew."

Friend snuggled next to her, knowing that something was wrong.

CHAPTER THIRTY

Dinner was ready, and Ag Leh was called to the table. There were usually only three dinner settings, but this evening, there was a fourth.

Ag Leh took her place at the table and waited.

Yin Yin and Yang Yang entered with a very old man with a white beard that reached his waist. He was wearing a black silk jacket and pants that had gold embroidery with traditional Chinese symbols.

"Ag Leh, this is our guest for the evening, Doctor Oh," Yin Yin said pleasantly.

Ag Leh nodded, and the doctor nodded back.

"Doctor Oh will be joining us for dinner and for a short time after," Yin Yin said.

Yang Yang served the meal and poured the tea for everyone. The conversation was light and was about local news, the weather, and talk about a new train track that was being built for the workers to travel into the city.

After dinner, they all retired into the living area.

"I understand that you did not pass your final dragon slaying test today, Ag Leh," Doctor Oh said in a concerned voice.

"You are correct," Ag Leh replied.

"I also understand that you passed everything else. That you have a wonderful ability designing and then braiding the handles of the katana sword."

"I enjoy braiding, and everyone appreciated the workmanship that I do," she replied.

"I also understand that you have a natural ability of finding flaws in the sword so they may be corrected. You are a very talented young woman. I wish you the best in your future."

With all of that praise, why was he so concerned about her future? Ag Leh thought.

"Ag Leh, we have decided that you can no longer stay with us because you failed to do what we directed you to do. We contacted the headmaster of the orphanage, and he said he does not have room for you to return at this time," Yang Yang said in a quiet but stern tone. "The good Doctor Oh is going to give you a medicine this evening at bedtime that will change your future.

"We have decided that you will wake up tomorrow morning in an orphanage in the country of

Sweden. You will have a new name: Helga. You will know your surroundings, and you will be able to speak the language. You will need to report to the office of the secretary of the orphanage first thing in the morning. You will receive your new life papers, which you must safeguard with your soul. You will be welcomed by the other children, and you will find happiness in your new life."

"What if I don't want to go? Do I get a say in this matter?" Ag Leh said, even knowing that this showed more disrespect for everyone in the room.

"This is what we have decided, and this is your new future," Yang Yang said.

"You will be very happy there," Doctor Oh said. "The Swedish people are the kindest people in the world."

"Go to your room now and say good-bye to Friend. We will be there in a couple of minutes," Yin Yin said.

Ag Leh thought about escaping outside of these prison walls, but she knew they would catch her so she went directly to her room.

She told Friend that after tonight, she would never see him again and hoped that they took good care of him. Friend just snuggled up against her.

Ag Leh lay in her bed, and Yin Yin, Yang Yang, and Doctor Oh entered.

Doctor Oh walked over to her with a glass of tea and a pill.

"Please take this pill. Tomorrow morning you will awaken in a new land of happiness where there are no dragons to slay," Doctor Oh said and handed her the tea.

Ag Leh took the tea in one hand and the pill in the other and swallowed both. She leaned back and laid her head on her pillow and closed her eyes, knowing that she would never see Friend again.

Chapter Thirty-One

Ag Leh opened one eye and then the other as the sun streamed onto her face. She sat up in bed; she was surrounded by whitewashed stone walls with large windows that let in the morning light.

She touched her blanket, and it felt rough to the touch. She thought she remembered silk down comforters. She looked around; she was in a room full of rose-cheeked blond girls. They were also waking up and getting dressed in their skirts and blouses.

Everything seemed normal but strange at the same time. Helga had no memory of her past but was aware only of the present.

"Helga, get up. It's morning and breakfast is in thirty minutes," the girl in the bed beside said.

Helga rubbed her eyes. She felt like this was her home, but she was disoriented at the same time.

In the back of her mind, she kept thinking that she needed to visit the secretary's office. She got out of bed, put on the clothes at the foot of her bed and headed to the secretary's office.

The secretary's office door was open, and sitting at the desk was a lovely older woman with her blond hair wound around her head in a bun on top of her head.

"Good morning, Helga. Your paperwork is in this envelope," the secretary said as she handed her the envelope with Helga spelled in very large letters. "If you need anything, you just come to me, and I will help you. It's not easy losing your parents in a boating accident and you being the only survivor. I have never had such an experience, but I can truly feel your pain."

"Thank you, ah…" Helga said with a long pause.

"Viktoria. My name is Viktoria," the secretary replied.

"Thank you, Viktoria. You are very nice," Helga said as she turned and walked back to her dormitory.

She returned to her bed and opened the envelope. The other girls crowded around her to see what was in the envelope. She pulled out her official birth certificate, and there was her name Helga Sandberg. Then she pulled out papers about her previous schooling with grades. She finally pulled out a newspaper article about a family drowning in a boating accident, and the lone survivor was Helga Sandberg. She had not only lost her mother and her father, but she lost a twin sister and two brothers. She felt no emotion. It did not seem real.

Chapter Thirty-Two

Helga created friendships quickly. She had a great grasp on the language and picked up local customs quickly too. Life seemed to be great in Sweden.

Sweden government cared about the welfare of all of its residents, including the orphans. The orphanages were well staffed to educate the orphans for a full life experience when they leave the orphanage. Food was plentiful, education was complete, plus each child learned the importance of contributing to the benefit of the whole group.

Helga enjoyed her new friends, her new teachers, and especially the staff that made her feel right at home from her first day.

The children would gather in the common areas and play games, and Helga was always included. She loved playing ball games with everyone. She made sure that she tried every sport at least once to see if she had the ability to play.

Winter arrived with vengeance; snow and ice covered everything within sight. The snow banks reached halfway up the windows of the cottages and stone homes. Pedestrians had to be careful where they walked because they had no idea what they might be stepping on.

Helga and the other children loved playing in the snow, throwing snowballs, making snow angels, sliding down the snow banks, and catching snow-flakes on their tongues.

"Mine tastes like vanilla," Helga said.

"Snow flakes don't taste," Wilma said with a laugh. "They are made of plain old water."

"Well, someone must have flavored mine then," Helga replied.

"I got a strawberry one," Julia screamed.

"See, they do come in flavors," Helga joyfully said.

The winter games had begun, and that was great fun for Helga.

CHAPTER THIRTY-THREE

Winter in Sweden brought short days and very long nights, with only six hours of daylight on the shortest days. That made eighteen hours of darkness that needed to be filled with studies and indoor activities.

But during the day, the children spend time out in the fresh air learning how to alpine ski and nordic skiing. Helga had difficulty with the alpine skiing because the speed and balance alluded her. She loved the nordic skiing because it was a slower pace, and she could take in the beauty of her surroundings. She watched in amazement at the speed that the nordic racers could achieve, but at this time, learning the skills of skiing was a lot of work. But skiing was the kind of work she enjoyed.

Helga would fall going down small hills, and she would laugh each time. She loved being cold and getting snow on her face. Her friends would help her up because they knew they would also be falling and need help getting up too.

Helga and her friends were on a nordic trail that encircled the orphanage, and the speed got the best of her. She slid off the trail over a bank and into a pile of snow that covered her. The boys and girls in the group took off their skis and jumped over the bank and dug her out of the snow mounds that encased her.

"Are you all right," Nova asked.

"I think so," Helga said as she shook her head and get the snow off her face. "I think so."

The children got Helga back onto the trail and got her boots attached to the bindings. The children got Helga back onto the trail with her skis and boots still attached.

"Ouch," Helga groaned. "Maybe I'm not okay. I think I did something to my ankle."

"Let's get that ski off," Ludwig said as he bent down to unbuckle the skis' bindings. "Hold on to my shoulder and neck, and we will get you back home. Someone pick up her skis. We have to get her to a nurse for a check up." He picked her up and carried her back to the orphanage. They visited the nurse's office.

"Yup, I think you sprained your ankle," the nurse said. "I don't think you did any real damage, but you need to rest and stay off that ankle as best that you can."

"I will do what you say."

The children got Helga back to her bed and pampered her for the rest of the evening, bringing her food, books, and her lessons for the next day.

Helga was happy that she had such great friends, and of course she knew she would have helped them too if they had problems.

CHAPTER THIRTY-FOUR

Within a couple of days Helga was feeling much better and was able to walk without pain. She went to the dining hall and saw Ludwig from a distance. she walked over to thank him.

"I would have done the same for anyone," Ludwig said. "I think I was born to rescue people. If I was born an animal, I guess I would have been a Saint Bernard dog, saving people in snow banks all over Sweden."

Helga laughed, and she knew that she just developed her first crush on a boy.

CHAPTER THIRTY-FIVE

Helga saw Ludwig almost every day in school, and they even studied together on the tougher subjects. It seemed that Helga knew the answers that Ludwig didn't, and he knew the answers to the questions she didn't know. They became very good friends.

They became part of the nordic ski team for the orphanage. They would practice together. They pushed each other to go faster. They practiced climbing the hills and then gliding down the other side of the hills.

Helga made friends with most of the children at the orphanage, and they enjoyed playing with Helga. Helga would also help other students with their studies. She just seemed to be a happy child.

There was a lot of excitement at the orphanage because the older children were going to have a trip to see the aurora borealis in northern Sweden. They were going to stay in cozy cottages close to the Abisko National Park, where the lake has its own microclimate called the blue hole.

The day arrived for the bus trip, and everyone had studied the phenomenon known as the northern lights. The science teacher had created charts, brought in pictures, and told them the scientific reasons for this natural wonder of the world.

Each cottage had enough room for six children and one chaperon. Meals were served family style in a dining hall; there was a building just for the bathrooms. Everyone settled in because they had to be ready to get up later in the evening for their viewing of the northern light.

The groups gathered at the bus, and the bus drove the short distance for the viewing spot in the blue hole over Lake Torneträsk.

The red, green, and purple lights played over everyone's heads. The streams of light seemed to dance like spirits, twirling, spinning, and leaping from hilltops to infinity. The lights were the most beautiful things that Helga had ever seen.

"I would love to live here someday," Helga said to Nova. "I would love to see this every evening in winter. It makes me very happy."

The group stayed at the cottages for three evenings enjoying the northern lights each night.

Then they had to return back to the orphanage, but Helga would dream about the beautiful sight of the aurora borealis.

Chapter Thirty-Six

The times of Helga's life flew by in an instant as it does for most people. She made many friends at the orphanage including the teachers, administrators, and the cooks.

Helga even offered to help the cooks in the kitchen, and the cooks really appreciated her efforts. Helga learned how to cook local foods, and her specialty was the fish from the lakes and the North Atlantic.

Graduation was fast approaching, and Helga was not looking forward to living on her own, so she and Nova decided that they would rent an apartment to share expenses once they got jobs.

Helga and Nova found jobs within days. Nova got a job in the office of the apartment complex they were living in, and Helga got a job at the Viking museum.

Helga quickly moved up the ranks on the museum staff and was especially interested in the weaponry of the Vikings. She gave tours of the museum, telling the tourist about the weapons and armor from 793 to 1066 AD. She explained that the weapon and the number of weapons showed others your wealth and status in the Viking community. A wealthy Viking would own one spear, two javelins, a wood shield, and a battle axe or sword. Helmet and armor were for the wealthiest of persons.

Helga found the Vikings a very exciting part of Sweden's history, and she had no idea why the weapons of war and death resounded so deep within her.

Every time she touched the blades of steel, her body trembled and at the same time delighted her.

CHAPTER THIRTY-SEVEN

Helga and Nova joined the Lutheran church for socialization aspect as much for the religion.

Helga was very personable and met almost everyone in the congregation. She met Britch, who lived with his parents and worked in maintenance for a local fishery.

Helga and Britch dated for about a year, and then they got married, and Nova was the very proud maid of honor.

They moved in with Britch's parent, but the quarters were cramped. Then Helga and Britch had their son Emong, so the quarters became even more crowded.

Helga still had dreams about the aurora borealis. In the mornings, she would tell her husband that she wished that at some point in their lives they could move to northern Sweden because she found the northern lights so beautiful and enchanting.

Britch came home from work one evening and said, "Helga, I have applied for and been offered a job near Tornetrask Lake, the lake you loved with the northern lights."

"I said I wanted to live there, and you found a job?" Helga asked.

"Yes, it is a handy man position at the cottages you stayed at," he replied. "We would get free housing in one of the cottages, and I would do the repairs and grounds work for them."

"That sounds great!" Helga said. "When does it start?"

"I need to give a two weeks' notice, and we could be there within the month," Britch said.

"I will miss your parents, but this is cramped for us and the baby," Helga said. "They won't be able to see their only grandson grow up, but we can't pass up this opportunity."

Two weeks later, Helga, Britch, and their son, Emong, were headed north on the train. This was Helga's and Emong's first trip on the train, and Helga was happily looking forward to living under the northern lights.

CHAPTER THIRTY-EIGHT

Helga, Britch, and Emong moved into their cottage. Britch needed rest to start his new job the next morning.

Britch woke up early and was looking forward to meeting the other employees and the guests. It is summertime, and the days are long, and the temperatures were comfortable.

Guests travel to Lapland for golfing under the midnight sun, swimming, sightseeing, hiking, horseback riding, and just the experience of twenty-four hours of sunlight.

Britch's jack-of-all-trades reputation got him this position, and he found out he needed to increase his numbers of trades. He had to recondition golf clubs because some golfers were too emotional and took their frustration out on the clubs. The rafts the swimmers used needed occasional repairs from over enthusiastic divers. The horse barns needed constant attention, and the guest cottages had to be checked daily for repairs. Britch was very busy with all his details.

Helga enjoyed her days taking care of her son in the great outdoors. This was something that they did not have in the city living in the cramped house with Britch's parents. Emong loved to crawl around in the grass, and then when he started to walk, he enjoyed the feeling of the grass on his feet. Helga was happy, Emong was happy, and that made Britch very happy.

One evening, as Britch arrived home, he walked toward Emong's room and saw Helga leaning over Emong's crib, sobbing.

"I can't do this," Helga was saying between her tears. "I don't want the responsibility of my child. I don't know if I am a fit mother."

Britch heard every word. Helga turned and saw her husband noticeably upset.

Helga went quiet and walked to the living room and sat down.

Britch went over to his son and gave him a strong hug, hoping that the young child did not understand what Helga had just expressed.

Chapter Thirty-Nine

Winter was fast approaching after a very pleasant summer. Soon the winter tourists will be arriving.

Helga took a job as a nordic ski instructor to occupy some of her hours.

If both Britch and Helga were working, they would put Emong into a daycare. Emong enjoyed meeting more children, and he especially liked the daycare providers. Everyone loved Emong as well.

Every night, during the winter, Helga and Britch would take their son out to view the aurora borealis. As the years passed, Emong became more excited when winter was arriving because he loved to see the dancing lights.

As the season cycled through the year, Helga's moods cycled with the hours of daylight. During the summer with total daylight, her moods were fine and level, but during the dark days of winter, she became violent and depressed.

One day, Britch approached his wife and asked if she wanted to move back to the city and his parent's house.

Helga, realizing that she sometimes had no control over her emotions, agreed to move back to the city with the understanding that they stay with Britch's parents only for a brief time.

The family returned to the city and moved in with Britch's parents.

Britch's parents were thrilled to see their grandson, who was now about seven years old.

Everything was fine for a while, but Helga was still dealing with her bouts of depression.

CHAPTER FORTY

Helga's depression appeared to be worsening, and Britch approached the minister of the Lutheran church for counseling. The minister suggested that maybe a change of location might help Helga deal with her mood swings and depression.

The minister said that the Lutheran churches in the United States were hosting families and finding them jobs and places to live, and the families only needed the cost of the fare for the steamships.

Britch, unknown to Helga, researched moving to the United States, and he was very pleased with what he read.

He contacted the minister; and Helga, Britch, and the ministers had a meeting about moving to the United States.

Helga was more receptive to the idea than either Britch nor the minister thought she would be, but the cramped living conditions with Britch's parents and the unsuccessful job hunt for Britch was discouraging.

The minister arranged for a Lutheran church in North Dakota to sponsor Britch and Helga.

Britch and Helga were excited about the prospects of moving to the United States with their young son. They both agreed that the opportunities had to be much greater in the United States.

CHAPTER FORTY-ONE

The family made the voyage to the United States on a steamship. It was a long, slow trip, visiting many ports, delivering and receiving cargo, but they finally saw the Statue of Liberty in the New York Harbor, and their hearts pounded with excitement.

Another chapter was about to begin. A new beginning. A new life. A new home. A new career. New happiness.

A person holding a sign bearing their names met them on the pier. He took them to his vehicle, and he told them that they were headed to North Dakota, but first he had to visit a couple of Lutheran churches in New England, the northeastern section of the United States.

With each stop at a Lutheran church, they were greeted with kindness and respect. They were given a place to sleep in a home of one of the Lutherans, and the congregation brought food to the meeting with their sponsor. Helga, Britch, and Emong enjoyed meeting with Lutherans from New England.

When they were in Connecticut, a fellow Lutheran gave them a picnic, and the family enjoyed a meal on the park beside the local Lutheran church.

They were enjoying their meal when Britch took a hard swat at a bug that crawled up his pant leg. He didn't think much about it, but it would become a major medical problem later.

Their sponsor picked them up at the park and told them that he was requested to drive to Rutland, Vermont, to visit the Lutheran church to deliver some important papers. Britch thought that visiting Vermont was a great idea; since they arrived in New England, he had been reading the tourist information, and he was interested in seeing Vermont.

During their ride to Vermont, Britch started to feel ill, but he never noticed the red swelling that had developed on his leg from the tick bite in Connecticut. By the time they reached the Lutheran church in Rutland, he could barely move. His entire body ached, and moving caused him excruciating pain.

At the Lutheran church, the sponsor who was driving Helga and her family to North Dakota spoke with the local pastor, and he told him about Britch's health issues and didn't think that Britch would make the long ride to North Dakota.

The pastor suggested that Helga and her family stay with him and his family for a little while until they could find some place suitable for them and a job, but with Britch's failing health, the prospects for a job did not look promising.

The sponsor left Helga, Britch, and Emong in the care of the pastor and he drove alone to North Dakota.

The pastor had a dinner gathering in Britch and Helga's honor, hoping that someone in the group would have an idea for Britch and his family.

One man from Tinmouth told him that he knew of a vacant place on Tinmouth Pond and thought that between the community of Tinmouth and the Lutheran church, it might be a good fit for the new family.

At the end of the meeting, that man gave the family a ride to Tinmouth Pond. He walked them through the wooded path to the sugar shack. It had been abandoned, but it was a roof over their heads.

Helga was not impressed with the accommodations, but thought that they would get better with time and with help.

Their lives on Tinmouth Pond had just begin.

CHAPTER FORTY-TWO

The whirl of four small propellers attached to the drone with a camera was the only sound that could be heard. The drone swooped down toward a hundred-year-old house on the dirt road that led to town.

The drone dropped down to the level of the front porch, and the camera turned toward the house and photographed the woman sitting on the porch sipping sweet tea, and then the drone flew up with the camera still filming the house.

"Cut!" yelled the director, and he slapped the script into his left hand. "Great job, Stella. That and the footage from this morning in the restaurant will make a great commercial."

Stella, still seated and sipping her sweet tea, grinned and said, "Good thing we got this thing wrapped up because I am headed to Vermont tomorrow morning."

"Vermont must be wonderful this time of year," the director said. "Got room for me in your suitcase?" he asked, laughing.

"Sorry, my suitcase is full, and I still have more to pack."

"You know, someday I will make my way up north and photograph landscapes, sunrises, sunsets, some of the natives of Vermont, and then spend a couple of weeks on Cape Cod," the director replied. "To think that I have never been out of the South."

"You would love the people and the landscapes," Stella said. "This year, I'm taking a friend with me for a month. That is the longest time that I will have ever spent in Vermont. Usually it is only a couple of weeks."

"Have a wonderful time in the Green Mountain State," the director wished her. "I have seen the foliage photos and would love to see that in person. God's paintbrush at his finest."

"I am excited to show my friend, Thelma, what I know about Vermont. It will be a great vacation, and I get to see my friends of Tinmouth Pond," Stella said. "They are some of the finest people on earth."

"Have fun," the director said. "I need to get this commercial edited and to the TV station. See you at the restaurant when you get back."

CHAPTER FORTY-THREE

Helga was washing dishes at the kitchen sink, looking out over Tinmouth Pond. She watched as a fish jumped and then splashed back, causing ripples across the water.

A powerboat zoomed by with tubers screaming their lungs out.

A kayak glided by close to the shore.

The sun was out with a gentle breeze. Just a perfect day at the pond.

A reflection in the window over the sink disturbed Helga. Two figures had just walked by the camp on the road. One figure was dressed in a silver robe, and the other figure was dressed in a gold robe.

A shiver went down her spine.

Helga ran to the door, and she watched as the pair crested a knoll and were gone.

CHAPTER FORTY-FOUR

Stella sat on her front porch, reading a book about the spiritualist living in Vermont in the 1880s. She had just reached the chapters about the Eddy brothers from the town of Chittenden, a short ride north of Tinmouth Pond.

She became transfixed when she got to the part about William and Horatio Eddy going into a trance and having spirits appear and speaking in foreign languages, which neither brother would have ever known.

Spiritualism was alive and well in the mid-1870s in Vermont and around the world.

The Eddy brothers and their mother opened the Green Tavern where people from around the world would stay and attend the nightly séances.

The abuse the Eddy brothers endured was very upsetting to Stella.

Stella was brought back to the present by the noise of the bus roaring down the dirt road.

The bus came to a complete stop in front of Stella's porch; the driver got out of the bus and opened the compartment under the bus to retrieve two small suitcases and a pink bowling ball bag.

Thelma emerged from the bus in full regalia. Dressed as if she had chosen her clothes from many different closets, Thelma walked toward the porch, smiling at Stella. Stella stepped off the porch, and the two women hugged each other tightly.

"Thelma, your bags. Your bags are ready," the bus driver called, and Thelma turned around and retrieved her bags.

The bus driver got back into the driver's seat of the bus and continued his trip down the dirt road.

"This is going to be a great vacation," Stella said. "I can't wait to see your reaction of the mountains of Vermont and the fresh, crisp air."

"I'm all excited too," Thelma said. "I've been reading about Vermont and can't wait," Thelma noticed the book in Stella's hand. "What are you reading?"

"A book about the spiritualist movement in Vermont in the 1870s," Stella said. "I am sure that you will be very interested, and we might be able to visit their old homestead."

Stella motioned for Thelma to enter the house and offered her some sweet tea.

"We need to get to bed early because tomorrow we start our journey to Vermont," Stella said.

The two women settled in for the night because tomorrow morning was coming soon, and the trip to Vermont is a long ride.

CHAPTER FORTY-FIVE

On the shore of Tinmouth Pond, Big Clint and Little Clint were sitting on the bench on the dock.

"Can I ask you a question, Gramp?" Little Clint asked.

"You, young man, can ask me anything anytime," his grandfather replied. "I am here to give you my years of wisdom."

"Why are we here?" Little Clint asked.

"We are here because Tinmouth Pond is such a great place to spend our summers. Spending precious time with our family and friends," Big Clint said.

"No, I mean a bigger *here*. Like why are we even on earth," Little Clint said.

"That has been the question asked by millions of people throughout time," his grandfather said.

"Well, why are we here?" Little Clint continued.

"I think we are here to be good people. We are here to help others and make others happy. We are here to take care of our families and to help friends and others. We are here to pass our wisdom down to the next generation. I think it is a spiritual thing," Big Clint said. "We need to make every day a good day. And we probably can't think too hard on the subject because I don't know if there is a finite answer."

"I guess I understand," Little Clint said.

"We just need to do our best every day so that there are no regrets at the end of life," Big Clint said. "Yeah, I guess we need to make the world a nicer place to live and have no regrets.

"Did I ever mention to you"—Big Clint looked north up the pond—"that that mountain range over there looks like a sleeping dragon? See, the dragon's body from his rump to his resting head and then his tail curls around him."

"I see it, I really see it," Little Clint replied excitedly.

"See where the eye is?" Big Clint asked.

"Yeah!" his grandson nodded.

"The eye looks like he is sleeping during the summer, but when autumn arrives, that area of trees is a different color, and it looks like he is looking out over Tinmouth Pond," Big Clint said. "It looks like he is surveying the whole area to make sure that we are safe for the coming winter. It is an amazing sight. To think we have a dragon living in the pond and also a mountain range of a dragon."

"Gramp, I am so happy to have you as my grandfather," Little Clint said. "You are a special person to me and to the world. You make everything an event, every day special, and you make Gram happy too."

The two men sat on the bench quietly, thinking about their conversation and looking at Dragon Mountain.

"Dinner's ready!" Little Clint's grandmother yelled from the camp. "Come and get it."

"If we want to keep her happy, we better get up there," Big Clint said, and they walked up the lawn to the camp for dinner.

CHAPTER FORTY-SIX

"You ready to head to Vermont?" Thelma asked Stella.

"I think I've got everything out here on the porch," Stella said as she turned to lock the door.

"Good because the bus is coming down the road," Thelma replied.

It was the same bus driver that dropped Thelma off the day before.

"You ladies ready to venture to Vermont?" the bus driver said as he descended the bus steps.

"We sure are," Stella said.

The bus driver put the suitcases in the compartment, and each woman carried on her purse and a bag of snacks.

"I will get you to the train station in no time, and then you will be headed north," the bus driver said as they all took their seats.

It was only an hour ride to the train station, and the bus driver got off the bus, unloaded the luggage from under the bus. When they arrived, he gave the ladies their bags and he wished them a safe and happy journey.

"My bowling bag!" Thelma yelled.

The bus driver retrieved the pink bowling bag from under the bus and handed it to Thelma.

Thelma thanked the bus driver

"He really is a great guy," Thelma said to Stella.

"He's also a great tipper at the restaurant," Stella replied.

The two adventurers made their way to the train ticket window, bought their tickets, and waited on the platform for the train.

It was a short wait, and the train arrived. The journey has begun.

CHAPTER FORTY-SEVEN

Twenty-five hours later, the lady travelers arrived in New York City, but they didn't have enough time to get in any sight seeing because they had to catch the train to Rutland, Vermont.

"Wow, we have seen a lot of the United States on this trip," Thelma said. "It is amazing how the landscape changes as you move around this country."

"It has been a long ride, but the train was comfortable," Stella replied. "And now onto Vermont."

The last leg of the trip was only five hours. As they were approaching the Rutland train station, they couldn't contain their excitement.

"Get ready for some really fresh air," Stella said. "And to meet Big Clint.

The train came to a stop at the platform, and the ladies gathered their bags and proceeded to get off the train. Standing right in front of them as they stepped from the train car was Big Clint.

Stella hugged Big Clint and introduced Thelma.

"Very pleased to meet you, Thelma," Big Clint said. "I hope you enjoy your first visit to Vermont.

"Thank you," Thelma said. "I am sure we will have a great time."

Big Clint helped the ladies put their bags into his truck, and they all climbed into the truck. Thelma grabbed her pink bowling ball bag and kept in nestled in her lap.

"This truck sure is an antique," Thelma said. "What fun to ride in this truck."

"It still runs great even thought it's a little rusty," Big Clint said. "We'll be at Tinmouth Pond in about thirty minutes. Everyone is waiting to see you, Stella, and to meet Thelma.

"So you're a bowler, Thelma?" Big Clint asked.

"No. Why do you ask?" Thelma replied.

"Because of the bowling bag," Big Clint replied.

"No, I carry my crystal ball in the bowling bag because it fits," Thelma replied. "And I never leave home without it."

"Crystal ball?" Big Clint questioned.

"Yea, I want to know my future, and sometimes I have questions for it," Thelma said.

"What do you do for a living?" Big Clint asked with great interest.

"I have a little boutique in New Orleans," she replied. The engine of the old truck sputtered, so she spoke louder. "I sell lots of things like crystal balls, séance stuff, potion ingredients, and just about anything that any Wicca would want."

"Very interesting, but a little bizarre for me," Big Clint said, knowing that he also had some very special bizarre secrets of his own. "Then you will fit right in with Vermont and Vermont's history," Big Clint continued. "There has been a lot of strange happenings in these hills from the beginning of time. We had the Eddy Brothers and their mother in Chittenden who contacted dead people and also stories of Indian villages that had been seen and then amazingly vanished into thin air."

"I read about the Eddy Brothers," Stella said. "But I didn't know about the Indians villages."

"Yes, some people claim they saw Indian villages in the woods in Chittenden. They placed a rock to mark the spot that they were there and went into town to bring back their friends. But they found that rock and the village had vanished," Big Clint said. "Very mysterious and also fascinating."

"There really is a lot for me to work with in this wonderful state," Thelma said as her mind started whirling about with thought of what she might find within the next month.

Big Clint drove his old truck up the mountain road to Tinmouth Pond and delivered the ladies to their cottage on the pond. A metal sign of a moose and the words "Ber-Bur Lodge" was hanging on the remains of an old tree.

"There you are, Thelma," Big Clint said as he applied the brakes. "This is your cottage for the next four weeks. It's small but has two bedrooms and is very comfortable, and we're just up the road."

"It looks very nice," Thelma said. "And I love the sign."

Big Clint took the bags and led the ladies into the cottage.

"This is beautiful," Thelma said, "and a view of the pond. This is going to be fun, and to know our neighbors is a plus."

Big Clint left the ladies to unpack, and Thelma picked up her pink bowling bag and placed her crystal ball on the table in front of the window.

"I bet the crystal ball gives us some answers about Vermont this week," Thelma gushed as she peers into the crystal ball. "I'm getting more excited 'bout this vacation every minute that I'm here. I feel something magical about this area, this pond, and this state."

"Hopefully your magical moments will be all that you wish for," Stella said. They sat down in easy chairs, putting their feet on a footrest, and just enjoyed the view out the windows.

CHAPTER FORTY-EIGHT

"Mom, what's wrong?" Emong asked his mother as he entered the house.

"I don't know," Helga responded, but she was noticeably shaken.

"There's something upsetting you," her son said.

"I was washing the dishes a couple of days ago, and I saw a reflection of two figures, one dressed in a gold robe and the other dressed in a silver robe. I went to the door and watched them walk up the road," Helga said. She sat on a stool because she became a little weak. "I don't know why, but I feel like I must know them from somewhere, but I have never seen anyone dressed like them. Now I think I just caught them out of the corner of my eye, and they wandered into the woods." Helga's face became flushed.

"Why are you concerned?" Emong asked as he watched her face go pale.

"I don't know why I am concerned, but I get a queasy feeling in my stomach," Helga said as she rubbed her stomach. "Just an odd feeling, and I have never seen them around the pond or around the village. I just don't know."

"When you see them again, just give me a yell, and I will follow them and find out where they go," Emong said with concern. He knew his mother had spells of being upset, but this time, it was different like she had seen a ghost or something.

Emong left the house, and the screen door slammed as he left. Emong had to take care of their lawn, and he had promised to mow two other lawns after that.

Chapter Forty-Nine

"Any place you ladies would like to visit?" Big Clint asked Stella and Thelma the next morning.

"Do you know where Chittenden is?" Stella asked.

"Of course I do," Big Clint replied. "It'll probably take about an hour to get there from here."

"We would like to visit the Eddy brothers' homestead," Thelma said. "We have done a little detective work on them and would like to visit their home and maybe ask some townspeople if they knew them even though they died back in the late sixties"

They loaded themselves into the truck.

"Does you wife want to join us?" Stella asked.

"No, she's practicing a Christmas cookie recipe that she is trying to perfect," Big Clint said. "She loves to bake and find new recipes from around the world."

"Christmas cookies? It's only the beginning of July," Thelma questioned.

"We'll have July cookies when we get back," Big Clint said with a jolly laugh.

Little did Thelma and Stella realize that Santa Claus was chauffeuring them to the town of Chittenden.

Thelma was amazed with the beauty of Vermont. She loved seeing the cows in the fields eating grass. She saw the farmers bailing up hay for the winter. She saw signs that read "Maple Syrup Sold Here" everywhere.

"What is maple syrup?" Thelma asked.

"It is a delicacy from boiling down the sap from the maple trees. It is sweet and pure gold in these hills. It goes on pancakes, ice cream, into cooking and baked beans," Big Clint said.

"Maybe we will have to try some," Thelma said.

"We have some back at camp, and we will make breakfast for you with real Vermont maple syrup," Big Clint said because he really enjoyed making pancakes in the morning.

"There's a sign that says Chittenden," Stella said. "The homestead is just before a large cemetery on the left side of the road. There, there it is. It has to be the house because that house had been built in the 1800s. And the cemetery is just up the road. That has to be the spot."

Big Clint pulled the truck into the driveway and said, "Let's get out and walk around. It's now a ski lodge."

"You wonder if we'll see spirits or ghosts?" Thelma said in anticipation of something big was going to happen.

Big Clint put the truck in park, and the three stretched their legs and walked around the outside of the house.

The house is an old farmhouse similar to the house Stella lives in in Mississippi. The front porch is the entire width of the front of the house and has rocking chairs in a tidy row.

"This is great to see this place. I don't feel anything, but it is still great to be here, and the day is still young," Thelma said. "Maybe we can find someone to talk to about the Eddy brothers."

They got back into the truck and continued their journey up the road and they came to an old country store.

"Maybe someone at the store knows something about the Eddy brothers," Thelma said.

Big Clint pulled the truck into the store's parking lot, and the three entered the store. They picked up some drinks.

"Hi, I'm Thelma, this is Stella, and this is Big Clint," Thelma said to the elderly man, who was petting the store's gray cat.

"I am Ralph," the man replied.

"Can you tell us anything about the Eddy brothers?" Stella asked.

"I went to a séance once at the Eddy brothers' home, and it was very interesting," the man said. "If you can stay around for a bit, I get off work in an hour, and I can show you around some," Ralph said.

"That would be great," Thelma said, all excited.

"Meet me back at the Eddy brothers' place in an hour," Ralph said, "I am sure you will enjoy hearing my story."

Thelma thanked him and said that they would be at the Eddy brother's homestead in exactly sixty minutes.

The trio continued up the road and accidently found another cemetery next to the center of the tiny village.

"Let's visit that cemetery," Thelma suggested.

Big Clint drove into the cemetery; it was extremely quiet. He didn't even hear any birds or even the wind.

The three wandered around looking at headstones.

"Some of these markers are beautiful," Stella said. "The engravings are great. This is a very old cemetery. Look at the dates."

And then they were stopped in their tracks because one headstone read William Eddy of Chittenden and another read Horatio Eddy of Chittenden.

"We found their graves," Thelma said. "And we weren't even looking for them. I bet we'll learn a lot from Ralph this afternoon."

Chapter Fifty

Big Clint, Stella, and Thelma were at the Eddy Brothers homestead before Ralph got there. They sat on the tailgate of the truck and enjoyed the sun and the breeze.

Ralph showed up as he promised.

"Glad you stayed in town," Ralph said. "I have a great story for you. You have seen the house, but I want to take you across the road to Honto's cave where many séances were held."

Ralph led the way through the woods until they came to a small ravine with high banks. At the head of the ravine were large boulders that had fallen onto themselves, and people referred to it as Honto's cave even though it was rocks with water running through it.

"This is where I attended a séance once," Ralph said. "I joined a group from Connecticut, a man from Rutland who believed in the Eddy brothers, a medium, a couple of my friends joined me, and we all came to this spot.

"I am not able to see dead people, but my friend said that he was a seer. The medium sat down in the ravine on a dry spot, and she had a tape recorder with her. We could not hear her, but we would listen to the tape later over dinner. My friend said that there were two Indian chiefs over on the other bank," Ralph said as he pointed to the other side of the ravine. "And they were on horseback. They were speaking to each other in a Morse code language, my friend said. He had no idea what they were saying, but it sounded like Morse code to him. He thought they were friends and discussing the situation of their tribes. After the medium was done, we returned to the house, and later we listened to the tape. The medium said the same thing my friend said, and over her voice, you could hear a Morse code sound. It was very surprising to me and my friends."

Thelma was thrilled with this story and hung onto every word that Ralph said.

"It was quite a day for me because that evening, we had a séance in the house, and that was the first time that I had ever let myself go into a trance. I felt like I was giving my energy to the medium who was thrashing on the floor beside me. It was interesting but also a little scary," Ralph said.

"And over there in the woods," Ralph said as he pointed, "is a clearing that some local townspeople claim that they saw an old Indian village, but when they returned, the village had vanished as if it had never been there."

Stella stood there amazed.

Big Clint listened to every detail, and he enjoyed the way Ralph told his stories.

"It has been said that this is a very sacred place for American Indians, and that is why people get different feelings, sensations, or visions," Ralph kept going.

"Do you believe in these stories?" Thelma asked.

"No reason not to believe in them," Ralph replied. "Strange things do happen, so why wouldn't they happen in Chittenden?"

The four walked back to the house.

"We cannot thank you enough, Ralph, for our tour and all of your insight. You have made this a great day for all of us," Thelma said.

"Thank you," Stella and Big Clint said.

"This was great fun for me too," Ralph said as he hugged Stella and Thelma and he shook Big Clint's hand.

"Big Clint, are you psychic?" Ralph asked Big Clint.

"No, I'm just an old farm boy from Vermont," he replied.

"Funny I got a feeling that you are someone special," Ralph replied. "And my instincts are pretty good."

Ralph got into his car with his imagination running wild. He wondered who this Big Clint really was because he had sensations he had never felt before, and he knew that he had shaken hands with someone very, very special.

Everyone got into their cars and headed home.

"Ready for some Christmas cookies girls?" Big Clint said. "We'll have some in about an hour."

Chapter Fifty-One

"That was some story Ralph told us this afternoon," Thelma said on the ride back to Tinmouth Pond.

"That's one you can put into your book," Stella said.

"I'm not writing a book," Thelma replied.

"Not yet," Stella said with a chuckle.

"I found it very interesting, and to think that Chittenden is a sacred Indian area," Big Clint said. "You just never know what is over the next hill, around the next corner, or even in the waters of Vermont.

"There are a lot of interesting people in Vermont, and Vermont has been the birthplace of a lot of famous people like John Deere, Joseph Smith, US presidents Chester Arthur and Calvin Coolidge, plus Rudy Vallee. A pretty impressive list, if you ask me."

"We could spend years investigating Vermont's history. Maybe we'll never go home," Thelma said with a laugh, knowing that after about a month away from home, she will be glad to see New Orleans.

Chapter Fifty-Two

Helga heard a knocking on the screen door, and she answered it.

"Helga, do you remember us?" a figure in a golden robe asked.

Helga got sick to her stomach and said, "No. I have no idea who you are."

"We are from your past. A part of your life where you failed a very important test. We have been searching for you for many years and tracked you down at Tinmouth Pond," the figure dressed in silver said.

"What do you want from me?" Helga inquired with a quivering voice.

"We need your help to finish some business that you never completed," the gold robed person said. "We believe that you can help us accomplish a deed that we have been trying to complete for years. We think you know where the dragon we have been looking for is living. We think he is living in the pond right in front of your house."

"I don't know what you are talking about," Helga said.

"We will give you some time to think about it. Memories will come back to you," the figure in silver said through the screen door.

The two figures turned around and walked down the dirt road.

When Helga went to bed that night, she couldn't fall asleep. As she put her head on the pillow, all she could see was the two figures who talked to her through the screen door that afternoon.

Just as she fell asleep, Helga's dreams were frightening. Her first vision was of a village being devastated by a flood. She woke up screaming, and Britch asked if she was all right.

"I don't know," Helga said, "I just had a scary dream, and I don't know the meaning of it. It was a flood that destroyed an entire village that killed everyone. I don't know what it means."

"It probably means nothing," Britch said.

Helga didn't tell her husband that she had talked to two figures who wanted her help in finding a dragon in the pond.

Helga laid her head back on the pillow, but her mind never settled down enough to fall asleep. Visions of the flooded village, screaming people, the two figures in gold and silver, and a dragon reappeared in her wide-awake state.

CHAPTER FIFTY-THREE

Little Clint joined his grandfather on the dock.

"Gramp, what is one of the most important things one could ever learn?" he asked his hrandfather.

"Believe in Santa Claus!" Big Clint responded without hesitation.

"Do you believe in Santa Claus?" his grandson asked.

"Of course I do," Big Clint said, knowing that he was the ultimate answer of who is the real Santa Claus.

"Why?" Little Clint asked.

"Because if you believe in Santa Claus, then you believe that anything is possible. There are Santa Clauses around you every day doing gesture for people they don't even know. Everyone is Santa Claus and have Santa Claus's spirit every day of their lives. Everyone should be making life fun for everyone around him or her every day," he said.

"I'll tell my friend Pee Wee that, because he wonders if Santa Claus exists," Little Clint said.

"Tell Pee Wee that if he had the spirit of Santa Claus," Big Clint continued, "he would be surrounded by Santa Claus all day long."

Little Clint sat watching the sunset, wondering about Santa Claus.

Chapter Fifty-Four

Little Clint went to visit Stella and Thelma because he had some news that he had just heard on the radio.

Little Clint knocked on the wooden door. He heard someone say "Come in."

He entered the cottage, and the two ladies were enjoying their breakfast.

"Miss Stella and Miss Thelma, I just wanted you to know the news that just came over the radio," Little Clint said. "There was a prison break about two hours from here, and they want people to call the police if they see anything strange. I don't think they'll come to Tinmouth Pond, but just in case."

"That's alarming," Thelma said. "We'll take precautions, and of course we are usually together anyway. We can take them. We're good old gals from the south,"

Stella had a nervous laugh and said, "Thanks, we will let you and the police know if we see anything odd around here."

"How about some brownies to take home? We just made them," Stella continued. "I love to bake but not as much as your grandmother. Have her try some of our southern walnut brownies."

"Thanks, I'm sure she'll like them," Little Clint said as he left the cottage.

CHAPTER FIFTY-FIVE

Little Clint didn't go to his grandmother's but instead decided to visit Timmy, the Tinmouth Pond Monster, in the pond.

Little Clint went to the end of the dirt road and sat on the bank of the pond and waited to see if Timmy would see him. Pretty soon, Little Clint saw the scales on Timmy's back appear, and then he saw the top of Timmy's head. Timmy didn't swim toward Little Clint the way he usually did. He seems to just float, and he didn't put his head out of the water. Little Clint was concerned.

Timmy finally got to the shore and lifted his head to greet Little Clint, and he looked exhausted.

Little Clint looked into Timmy's eyes, and they were dark and lifeless.

"What's wrong?" Little Clint yelled as he jumped to his feet, but there was no response from Timmy.

Timmy just lay in the water, tired and weak.

Little Clint turned around and ran to his grandparent's house.

Little Clint got to his grandparents' cottage and barged through the door yelling, "Gramp! Gramp! Timmy is very sick. He wouldn't even stick his head out of the water for me. I don't know what is wrong with him."

Big Clint grabbed his grandson's hand, and he loaded him into his truck, and they drove to the end of the road.

Big Clint got out of the truck with his grandson, and he saw Timmy just lying in the water.

"Quick, we need help," Big Clint said. "Get back into the truck."

They drove back to the cottage, and Big Clint called Mr. Baker, the log truck driver.

"Mr. Baker, this is Big Clint at Tinmouth Pond. Can you do us a great favor and come up here immediately with your logging truck, and bring straps. I'll explain when you get here," Big Clint said. "We will be at the end of our road." There was a pause, and Big Clint said, "Thanks. See you shortly."

He then dialed another number.

"Dr. Bruce please," Big Clint said. "Dr. Bruce, we have a real emergency. Can we get an animal into your office in about hour? We can? We will be there in about an hour. Thanks." He hung up the phone.

"Let's get back to Timmy," Big Clint said. "Maude, you come with us. We may need extra hands."

Big Clint, his wife, Maude, and grandson got in the truck and returned to Timmy.

"Oh my goodness," Maude said. "He is very, very sick. Good thing you have a logging truck coming because how else could we get him to the veterinarian."

Soon the sound of the logging truck coming up the road was heard.

Mr. Baker got out of the truck, but he didn't see an emergency.

"What is going on, Big Clint?" Mr. Baker asked. "I don't see anything for my truck to pick up."

"Mr. Baker, I have to tell you a secret that is just between us. We have a dragon out there about fifteen feet from the edge of the water," Big Clint said.

Mr. Baker looked out into the water, and he saw nothing.

"If you agree to help load him onto your truck, you will instantly see Timmy the Tinmouth Pond monster. If you don't want to help, then you will not see him," Big Clint told Mr. Baker.

"Of course I will help," Mr. Baker said, and then instantly he saw Timmy lying in the water, tired and weak. "Let me get the tie downs and turn the truck around."

Mr. Baker turned that huge truck around and backed up to the pond. He lowered the boom out over the water. Big Clint and Little Clint got into the water and tied the ropes around Timmy. Mr. Baker extended the boom arm out over the water. They tied the ropes to the boom arm, and Mr. Baker slowly raised Timmy out of the water.

Mr. Baker was amazed when he saw this green dragon with purple wings emerging out of the pond. He slowly lowered Timmy onto the bed of the truck. Little Clint climbed up onto the bed of the truck and sat beside Timmy's head with Timmy's tail warped around his little human friend.

Big Clint got into the cab of the truck with Mr. Baker, and they headed to Rutland to see Dr. Bruce.

Maude watched as the logging truck lumbered down the dirt road, stirring up a lot of dust; she got into Big Clint's truck and drove home to wait for an update on the dragon.

CHAPTER FIFTY-SIX

Stella and Thelma were on the deck enjoying some sweet tea when they heard the sound of Mr. Baker's logging truck coming down the road.

Stella was curious, and she stood up and leaned over the deck's railing to see what was causing all the noise on this quiet afternoon.

"Thelma, come quick," Stella said. "Little Clint is riding on the back of the logging truck all by himself, and he is crying."

"What is going on?" Thelma asked. "There's nothing on the truck but one little kid."

"I don't know, but Big Clint's is in the cab, and he looks pretty upset too," Stella said. "Maybe something is wrong with truck. I don't see what else it could be. But they wouldn't be that upset over a truck."

"We'll just have to wait and see if we hear anything later."

CHAPTER FIFTY-SEVEN

Mr. Baker pulled into the animal clinic's parking lot, and an assistant who heard the truck ran to get Dr. Bruce from the examination room.

Dr. Bruce is known throughout New England as the world's best veterinarian. He is a small-framed man who looked like a mad scientist with his disheveled blond hair, but he is known for instantly knowing what is wrong with any animal.

The assistant told Mr. Bruce there was no animal on the truck, just a kid.

Dr. Bruce went out to the parking lot and introduced himself.

"Big Clint, I don't see an animal here. I hope this is not a hoax," Dr. Bruce said.

"This is not hoax," Big Clint said, and he turned to Mr. Baker to acknowledge his comment.

"Where is the animal you asked me to examine?"

"You have to promise not to tell anyone once I tell you, and then everything will become clear," Big Clint said.

Dr. Bruce agreed, and as he nodded his head, all of a sudden, a green dragon with purple wings appeared on the truck embracing Little Clint with its tail.

"I have never seen a dragon before," Dr. Bruce said. "And this is just amazing. What do you think is wrong with him?"

"We have no idea," Big Clint said. "We found him like this an hour ago in the water at Tinmouth Pond."

"First, we need to untie the ropes," Dr. Bruce said. "I need to get up on the truck."

Dr. Bruce had never touched a dragon nor had he ever looked into the eyes and mouth of a dragon.

Dr. Bruce climbed up onto the bed of the truck, and he grabbed Timmy's front foot to get leverage to get his balance. He stood up and looked into Timmy's eyes, and he saw a very tired and dis-traught animal.

"Get me a small ladder, please," Dr. Bruce requested.

Dr. Bruce's assistant had gone outdoors and heard the doctor's request and retrieved a small ladder from a shed, but the assistant still did not see any animal on the truck.

Dr. Bruce grabbed the ladder and placed it next to Timmy's mouth. "Open your mouth, Mr. Dragon," Dr. Bruce said.

"His name is Timmy," Big Clint said to him.

"Open your mouth, Timmy," Dr. Bruce said. "I'm coming in."

Dr. Bruce stood on the ladder and leaned into Timmy's mouth.

Mr. Baker, Big Clint, and Little Clint could see what was happening, but no one else could see anything but a kid and a veterinarian on the bed of the truck.

Dr. Bruce's assistant and everyone driving by saw Dr. Bruce on the ladder, and when Dr. Bruce entered the dragon's mouth, they just saw a pair of legs flailing in the air.

"I think I know what it is," Dr. Bruce yelled from inside Timmy's mouth. "There is a buoy blocking his methane chamber. I need something to grab onto the buoy with."

The assistant, still confused because he did not see an animal on the truck, found a hoe in the shed and ran to the truck and handed it to Dr. Bruce.

Dr. Bruce climbed back up the ladder and asked Timmy to open his mouth, and he slid back into the mouth of the creature that could have swallowed him whole. Dr. Bruce just hoped that Timmy didn't hiccup, inhale, or burp because he might just become toast.

He reached as far as his body would reach, and then he stuck the hoe down Timmy's throat and snagged the rope tied to the buoy with the blade of the hoe.

Very slowly he pulled the buoy out, and he backed out of Timmy's mouth. He stood on the ladder for a moment and took a deep breath. He looked into Timmy's eyes, and they looked brighter and full of life.

Dr. Bruce's assistant just stood in amazement as he saw his doctor first disappear into thin air and then appear on a ladder with a hoe and buoy. *Is this a magic act?* he thought as he rubbed his eyes.

"Dr. Bruce, we cannot thank you enough for saving Timmy," Big Clint said. "Without you, we would have a dead dragon on our hands."

"That was quite a thrill for me because I have never seen a dragon before," Dr. Bruce said.

"How did you know what was wrong?" Mr. Baker asked.

"Well, he looked despondent when I looked into his eyes, but everything else seemed normal except for his breathing, so I thought it has do something down his throat," Dr. Bruce said. "Then I thought that dragons breathe fire, and that fire would probably be produced by methane, and I didn't smell any methane so I thought that was an opportunity to see if his methane bladder was blocked. Then I saw a buoy down there, so that had to be the problem."

Just then Timmy raised his head skyward and blew a large flame of fire as appreciation to Dr. Bruce.

"I think that was a thank-you from the patient," Little Clint said. "Thank you, because I would be very upset if anything happened to Timmy."

"Young man," Dr. Bruce said to Little Clint, "you are the only kid I know that has a dragon for a friend." Dr. Bruce laughed and shook everyone's hands.

"Dr. Bruce, come up to Tinmouth Pond sometime to see Timmy in action," Little Clint said.

"That would be fun," Dr. Bruce replied. "But I probably can't use any of that information for a veterinarian journal because no one would believe me, plus I promised to never tell anyone. To think that I actually saved the life of a dragon."

"We would believe you," Mr. Baker said.

"Thanks, but no other veterinarian in the world has ever treated a dragon, so I am sure they would not believe me," Dr. Bruce said. "You better get Timmy back to the pond. I think he would feel much better there than listening to all of this traffic in Rutland."

They pulled out onto the road and headed to Tinmouth Pond.

Dr. Bruce walked back into the office, and his assistant caught up to him, and he said, "What just happened there?"

"Just a little magic and mystery," Dr. Bruce replied. "To tell you the truth, I was wondering the same thing."

CHAPTER FIFTY-EIGHT

Stella and Thelma heard Mr. Baker's truck roaring up the dirt road, and they looked out the window as he drove by.

"Well, everyone looked happier, but still nothing on the back of the truck except for Little Clint," Stella said.

"It sounded the same, so they didn't get the muffler fixed, I'll tell you that," Thelma replied with a laugh.

Mr. Baker took Timmy and the crew back to the lake and unloaded his cargo.

"Thank you, Mr. Baker," Little Clint said.

"We could not have done it without you and your truck," Big Clint said.

"You're welcome," Mr. Baker said.

"What do we owe you?" Big Clint said.

"How about some of the Christmas cookies your wife is known for," Mr. Baker replied.

"We'll get them to you by the end of the week," Big Clint said. "I didn't know her reputation had gone around the county."

"It has, and everyone can't wait for some Christmas cookies," Mr. Baker said as he climbed back into the cab of his truck.

CHAPTER FIFTY-NINE

"Where have you been, Emong?" Helga asked her son.

"I was walking around the pond," Emong replied. "Remember the pretty woman from Mississippi with the little dog? She is back for a month, but she left her dog with a friend in Mississippi. But she brought her friend named Thelma from New Orleans."

"That's nice that she is back," Helga replied. "Maybe I should walk over and meet them soon. It would be nice to know more people."

"I would really like you to meet them. I think you need to get out more," Emong said.

"I'll think about it," Helga said.

"Don't think too long. They are only here for four weeks," Emong said with a laugh. "Blink, and they will back in Mississippi."

CHAPTER SIXTY

There was a knock at the door of Stella's cottage.

"Thelma, can you get the door?" Stella said. "I'm up to my elbows in cookie dough."

Thelma went to the door, and there were two men who pushed by her and entered the cottage.

"Got any money, ladies?" the older stockier man said. "We need money now."

"No, we don't," Thelma said.

"Well, you better find some," the younger taller man yelled.

"We just broke out of prison, and we need money and food," the older one said.

"We murdered people that didn't give us money, and we will do it again if we have to," the younger man said.

Stella was stunned, and she wondered how they were going to get out of this situation. She reached up into the cabinet and accidently poured laxative powder into the cookie dough.

"I have some brownies and shortly will have some cookies ready," Stella said.

"They don't have walnut, do they?" he said, "I'm allergic to walnuts."

"No, they don't have walnut. I'm allergic to walnuts too," Stella said.

"Got any milk?" the older murderer growled.

Thelma retrieved milk from the refrigerator.

He chugged the milk from the carton.

"You should have better manners than that," Stella said to him firmly with her Southern drawl.

"Really, old lady? You think I worry about manners," the older guy said.

"It's just a nasty habit. If you do that all the time, you could give your friend here a cold or cold sore or something," Stella said without thinking and decided she had better keep her mouth shut and continued with her cookies.

Stella put the cookies in the oven and announced, "They'll be ready in twelve minutes."

"Good, I'm hungry," the young man said as he looked around for anything to steal. "What's that on the table? Is it worth anything?"

"It is a crystal ball," Thelma said. "And it's not worth anything to anyone except me."

"What do you do with it?" he asked.

"I see the future," Thelma said.

"Well, what's my future?" he said with a deep grunt.

Thelma walked over to the crystal ball, said a chant, and looked into the ball. She saw nothing.

"I see you living in Canada as a free man," she said, making it up.

"Really? That is where we are headed," he said.

"Don't tell them our plans," the older guy said. "You were the wrong person for me to break out of prison with. Why don't you tell her the address you are headed to?"

"1376 West," the younger one said.

"Shut up! You really are stupid," the older man screamed.

"Cookies are done," Stella said. "Blow on them before you eat them. They are still hot."

The two men each took a hand full of the cookies.

"These are pretty good," the young man said.

"Thank you kind, sir," Stella said, trying to stay calm.

"Ah, my stomach hurts. I need a bathroom," the older guy said as he ran into the bathroom. "What did you put in those cookies?

"Nothing," Stella said.

"Hey, I'm breaking out in a rash, and I need a bathroom," the younger guy said.

"I'm in the bathroom," his friend yelled from the bathroom.

"You can go outdoors over there past the trees," Thelma said.

"Get out of my way, old lady," he said as he pushed past her on his way to the woods.

Just then, Little Clint was walking up the walk to the cottage.

"Call the police," Stella whispered to Little Clint.

"Why?" Little Clint asked.

"Don't ask, no time," Stella said.

Little Clint ran home and had his grandmother call the police.

"How you doing in there, sir," Stella asked through the bathroom door in her Southern drawl.

"You trying to kill me!" the man yelled back at her.

"I wouldn't do anything like that," Stella said back through the bathroom door.

"Stella, did you forget about the poison ivy in the woods when you sent him over there?" Thelma whispered.

"Nope. I remembered the poison ivy when I told him where to go," Stella said with a smirk.

The younger guy came back into the cottage. His lips were swollen, his eyes were bloodshot, and he had patches of rashes all over his head, neck, and arms. He then showed them little blisters on his ankles.

"What have you done to me?" the younger guy said. "I have diarrhea, I'm having a reaction like I had eaten walnuts, and now it looks like I have poison ivy," he said in a really mean voice. "You old ladies are evil."

The guy in the bathroom was still moaning and groaning.

"Did you have a weapon when you were here before?" Thelma asked the younger guy.

"Yeah, what did you do with it?" he asked.

"It might be in the poison ivy patch that you were just playing in," Thelma said.

"Get the gun for me," he yelled at Thelma.

"Glad to do it," she said.

Thelma found the gun and made sure she stayed away from the poison ivy.

Thelma entered the cottage with the weapon, and the younger man demanded she give it him.

"You think I'm as dumb as you are?" she said. "Now you sit down, be quiet, because us Southern girls know how to use a gun. Sit, I said. Sit, now!"

He complied like a puppy as she stood over him with the gun pointed at his head.

Off in the distance was the sound of a police cruiser.

"What's going on?" the man from the bathroom yelled.

"Your ride is coming," Stella said.

The cruiser stopped, and two policemen entered the cottage.

"We'll take it from here," the first officer said.

"Thanks, ladies," the other officer said.

"You old ladies are evil," the younger murderer said again.

"No more evil than you two," Thelma said.

"They have been exposed to poison ivy, so be careful, Officers," Stella said. "They both have diarrhea, and this one is allergic to walnuts. Just put down something to protect your car."

The two officers led the two escapees to the cruiser and drove off.

"Hey, make sure you spell our names right," Stella yelled as they drove away.

"What are you talking about, Stella?" Thelma asked.

"I'm sure we're going to make the papers with this one," Stella said.

Thelma agreed and hoped they were described in the paper as proper young ladies from the South.

CHAPTER SIXTY-ONE

The two figures in the silver and gold robes appeared at Helga's door again.

"Have you had time to think about what we said?" the figure in gold robe asked.

"I still don't know what you mean," Helga replied.

"Have you had nightmares?" he asked.

"Yes," she replied again.

"What were the nightmares about?"

Helga's voice shook. "The first was about a flood."

"Good, our spell worked. Your family was lost in a flood after a dam broke in China," he said.

"What are you talking about?" Helga asked in complete shock.

"You were born in China. We adopted you and taught you to work on swords. You braided the most beautiful sword handles that the world had ever seen. You were taught martial arts. We prepared you to be a dragon slayer, but you failed," the figure continued. "You failed your final test. We had you transported during your deep sleep to Sweden where you grew up and never remembered your past. We are here to have you slay that dragon you failed to kill many years ago."

"I have a family, and I am not a dragon slayer," Helga responded. "You need to go and leave me alone."

"We will never leave you alone now that we have tracked you down from the other side of the earth," the silver robed figure said. "We have searched everywhere for you and have spent our lives trying to kill a dragon. Once we get the dragon's horns and heart, we will be very wealthy and powerful."

"Dragons are mythical creatures. They don't exist," Helga said. "You two are insane."

"We know that the dragon we hoped to kill many years ago is living at the bottom of this pond," the figure in gold said. "We will get him, and we will get you to help us kill him."

With that, the two figures turned and disappeared into the woods.

An hour later, Emong decided to take a break from his lawn mowing duties and walked home for a drink. He walked into the camp, and Helga was slumped over with her head between her hands.

"Mom, what's wrong?" Emong asked.

"I don't know. I just don't know what to think is true or false. I don't know if I'm seeing things, hearing voices, or having a real conversation," Helga replied. "I saw those two figures again, and they are scaring me."

Emong hugged his mother's shoulder, and she began to relax.

Chapter Sixty-Two

Little Clint was loading the gnomes into the back of the pickup truck with his grandfather, and the sun was setting in the west.

"Little Clint," Big Clint said, "go get Stella and Thelma and then Emong and have them come over here as quickly as possible."

Little Clint ran to Stella's cottage and told them that his grandfather wanted to see them. Then he ran around the pond and got Emong to follow him.

Stella, Thelma, Emong, and Little Clint stood around the truck, and they noticed that the gnomes were all placed in tidy rows in the back of the truck.

"I was wondering if you wanted to go on an adventure this evening," Big Clint said to the group. We will take a little trip in my dear old truck to a party. But this is a very special night for the gnomes and myself, so you will only remember the beginning of the ride and our return. Even my grandson will only remember the beginning and the end."

"That is very enticing but also a little scary," Stella said.

"Sound like a lot of fun to me," Thelma said.

"I don't know about it," Emong said with a weary look on his face.

"Everyone will be fine, and this will be fun, but for certain reasons, you cannot remember the party part," Big Clint said. "It's not a bad thing, but there are certain secrets that have to stay a secret forever. So you can see a very great secret, but you just can't remember it."

"I'm ready to go," Little Clint said.

"Come on, Stella," Thelma began. "Get in the truck and let's see what happens."

"Come on," Big Clint said. "Get in, and we'll have a fun evening,"

Big Clint got into the driver's seat, Stella took the middle, and Thelma got the seat by the door. Little Clint and Emong climbed into the back of the truck and grabbed the sideboard, and the gnomes just sat where they were placed.

The truck chugged down the road and turned left onto Calvin Hill Road.

"Hold on tight," Big Clint yelled over the roaring engine. The truck started to climb the hill, and he pressed the gas pedal all the way to the floor. As they reached the top of the hill, the truck sounded like it was going to stall and slide backward, but the truck backfired and flew into the air, becoming Santa Claus's sleigh.

The gnomes came to life and started screaming with joy. Thelma and Stella had huge smiles on their faces, and the wind blew through their hair. Emong and Little Clint grabbed the sideboards tighter, looked at each other, and then laughed as loud as they could. The adventure had begun.

CHAPTER SIXTY-THREE

The sleigh filled with passengers was flying high over Tinmouth Pond. Heads were out of the windows to see the lights and reflections on the pond. The sun had almost set, and there was a mystical look to Tinmouth Pond. On the mountains, the lights of the farms were all aglow. Reflections of Rutland's lights reflected off the clouds to the north, and the light from Manchester were seen in the distance to the south.

"A beautiful sight," Big Clint said. "I love being up here in my sleigh."

"Your sleigh?" Thelma asked.

"This is the secret that you must never know," Big Clint said. "Now enjoy the ride because we are going go our annual gnomes party in Wallingford."

Big Clint and Farmer Russ brought all their gnomes together one night every summer so they can have a party on Dugway Road. Farmer

Russ enjoyed it just as much as Big Clint and all the gnomes.

"Look at the stars and the moon," Big Clint said. "This is a perfect night for the party."

"Where are we going?" Thelma asked.

"There is this very special spot on Dugway Road. It is like it fell from heaven," Big Clint said. "If you were driving Dugway Road, you would travel on a narrow dirt road between a ledge and a small brook, barely room for one car. And then you go around a couple of tight corners, and then all of a sudden, you come upon this very magical pull-off and the cutest spot you have ever seen."

"How did the parties start?" Thelma asked again, curious about this Dugway Road adventure.

"Farmer Russ and I both have our families of gnomes, and we thought we should bring them together once a year," Big Clint said. "The gnomes had so much fun that we thought we should do it every year. Get ready to hold on tight. The sleigh is going to descend," Big Clint said.

The sleigh started to reduce its speed and then started to descend back to the earth. The sleigh rocked side to side, and the gnome started screaming with excitement again.

The sleigh approached the treetops, and then it aimed for the dirt road. There in the distance was the pull-off of the road, and the passengers could see a steep hillside next to ledges and a brook right in the middle of everything. To the right of the pull-off is a road that cut through the ledge.

As the sleigh came to a stop, Big Clint said, "Dugway Road got its name because the old settlers dug their way through the ledge so the mail could be delivered."

On the banks were little campfires and lanterns hanging from the lower plants. There were gnomes on the other side of the brook having a grand time. Little Clint and Emong handed Big Clint the gnomes, and he placed the excited gnomes on the ground. The gnomes ran over the little bridge and joined their friends for the party of the year.

"Look how happy they are," Big Clint said as he watched all the gnomes hugging each other and starting to play games and dance.

Farmer Russ walked over, and Big Clint introduced him to his friends.

"I thought this was our secret," Farmer Russ said.

"They will not remember anything except being in the truck," Big Clint said.

"Great to see you, my friend," Farmer Russ said.

"What do you mean they will only remember the ride in the truck," Farmer Russ questioned.

"Their minds will only remember the ride in the truck," promised Big Clint.

"It is great to see you again too," Big Clint said. "It has been too long."

"Your family is fine, I hope," Framer Russ inquired.

"Everyone is fit as a fiddle, and yours?"

"Just a couple of minor things that we have overcome, so we are doing well," Farmer Russ said. "I just love seeing our gnomes come to life and have a great time. As long as they don't get into any trouble."

Stella and Thelma watched the antics of the gnomes, and the moonlight on the festivities took their breath away.

"This is a great spot. I'd like to see it in daylight, but it might not have all the charm that it has right now," Stella said.

"I bet it still has a special feeling, knowing that the gnomes have such a fun time here," Thelma said.

Emong and Little Clint crossed the rickety stick bridge to where the gnomes were playing. The brook was narrow enough that they could have straddled it, but they wanted to be part of the party and not seen as uninvited giants.

"Aren't they cute," Emong said, laughing.

"It would be fun to play hide and seek, but I am sure they would be able to find us," Little Clint laughed.

The evening was getting late, and the gnomes are not used to staying up too late, so Farmer Russ rang a bell to signify that the party was about to end.

Farmer Russ, with the help of Little Clint, loaded his gnomes into his wagon. Farmer Russ climbed into the buggy's seat and yelled to his team of draft horses, "Go home!" The horses seemed to know exactly what he meant, and off they went through the dug out ledge back to Wallingford.

Big Clint and Emong loaded Big Clint's gnomes back into the sleigh. The gnomes were still chattering, screaming, and laughing because they had such a great time. The gnomes were all yelling, "Thank you, Santa! Thank you, Santa."

"Santa?" Thelma asked.

"Yup, I'm Santa Claus," Big Clint said. "That is the secret that you cannot remember."

Thelma and Stella climbed into the front seat of the sleigh with Big Clint. Little Clint and Emong got into the package cargo area with the gnomes.

Big Clint turned the sleigh around, and the sleigh slid up the dirt road, gained a little speed, and all of a sudden, the sleigh was airborne. The ride back to Colvin Hill was more magnificent than the ride over. The ski was darker, the moon and stars were brighter, and the air was crisper.

"Take in that fresh air and all of the beauty of Vermont," Stella said as she leaned into Thelma as the sleigh took some sharp turned.

"This is like a rollercoaster ride," Emong said from the backseat.

"Yeah, just amazing," Little Clint said. "What a great night to ride the skies."

The sleigh was approaching Colvin Hill as it descended, and as soon as the sleigh's runners hit the dirt, the beautiful sleigh turned into the old rusty truck that they started their journey in. Everyone including the gnomes bounced in their seats as the sleigh hit the ground with a thud. The gnomes were now completely quiet and sat in their spots perfectly still.

The ride down the hill was just as exciting as the ride in the air due to its steepness. They made it back home, and everyone was laughing and talking about their ride. No one said a word about the ride in the sleigh or the party for gnomes because they did not remember anything except the ride in the truck.

Big Clint sent everyone home, and he unloaded his gnomes and placed them back into the garden. It was a long evening for him too, but he has had a lot of longer nights in his lifetime. Christmas Eve is a good twenty-four-hour ride because he has to encircle the whole world, making sure all the kids get their gifts.

CHAPTER SIXTY-FOUR

The next morning, Stella and Thelma gathered their coffee and muffins and walked out onto the deck and set their food and napkins on the table.

"That was quit a ride last night," Stella said.

"Yes, it was. But I am a little disoriented, I guess," Thelma replied.

"What do you mean?" Stella inquired.

"I looked at my watch when we left, and I looked at it again when we got home," Thelma said. "My watch said that we were gone almost three hours, but the ride up Colvin Hill and back down was only about thirty minutes." Thelma paused. "It just doesn't seem possible somehow."

"Maybe your watch is wrong." Stella said.

"It says 8:30 right now, and I believe it *is* 8:30," Thelma said. "I just don't know what to think, but it was a fun ride anyway."

They ate their muffins, drank their coffee, and took in the view of Dragon Mountain, not knowing that the dragon was watching them.

CHAPTER SIXTY-FIVE

Timmy and his friends stayed in the deepest part of the pond during the busiest part of the summer. The powerboat, the pontoon boats, and the fishing lines all caused problems for all the creatures living below the surface of the pond.

In a week or so, the summer rush of tourist would be over, and they would have returned to their homes. Timmy and his friends would be able to come up and see what was going on, but at that moment, it was better to be safe than sorry.

CHAPTER SIXTY-SIX

Little Clint was sitting on the dock in deep thought.

His grandfather joined him. "What are you thinking about, young man?" Big Clint asked.

"I made a mistake today," Little Clint replied.

"What kind of a mistake?" Big Clint continued his questioning.

"I was doing some summer homework for school, and I made a mistake, and Grammy found it," Little Clint replied.

"So what is the problem?" Big Clint continued.

"Well, I should never have made such a stupid mistake," replied the embarrassed grandson.

"Mistakes are learning tools."

"What do you mean, Gramp?"

"You will learn more from your mistakes than getting everything right the first time," Big Clint said. "Mistakes give you a chance to rethink your options. When you try different corrections, you will find happy mistakes. You will find something, and those somethings might lead you to something wonderful."

"Mistakes are a good thing?"

"Mistakes are a good thing if you use them as a good thing and not give up on your goals," Big Clint said. "Use your mistakes as a tool in your toolbox of learning."

They sat in the sun, looking at Dragon Mountain and taking in nature at its finest.

CHAPTER SIXTY-SEVEN

Maude was washing dishes as she watched her two favorite men sitting on the dock out the kitchen window.

Maude poured three glasses of lemonade and placed them on a tray and walked down to the dock.

"Gentlemen, would you like some lemonade?" Maude said to her husband and grandson.

"We would love some," Big Clint said.

Little Clint's grandmother sat down and handed them their drinks.

"Thanks, Grammy," Little Clint said as he took his lemonade.

"You know, I was thinking about Emong today" Maude said. "I think his little business is really taking off."

"Yeah, but he can't hang out with me because he is always too busy," Little Clint said sadly.

"You know," his grandfather said, "Emong has stick-to-itiveness, and that I really appreciate in a young person."

"Yes, he has goals, and he really tries to accomplish them," Little Clint's grandmother replied. "He is very determined for someone his age and from his upbringing."

"Don't I have stick-to-itiveness?" Little Clint asked.

"You do to a point," his grandfather said. "And you will be more goal-oriented as you mature and grow older. But right now, you want to have fun. And there is nothing wrong with having fun at your age."

"So what is stick-to-itiveness?" Little Clint asked.

"You have a goal," his grandmother said, "and you follow it through until you reach it, and then you look back at your accomplishment, and then you set a new goal. Emong has just got that stick-to-itiveness early."

"I have goals," Little Clint said.

"Yes, you do," Big Clint said. "And we are proud of you."

"But someday you will have goals for your life," his grandmother said. "And you will someday obtain your goals, and we will always be proud of you, whatever goals you desire," his grandmother asked.

"Little Clint, stick-to-itiveness will get you far in life," his grandmother said. "It is important to just show up and show that you are interested. The person who succeeds has reasonable goals, shows up to accomplish them, makes mistakes and realizes them, and sticks to their goals. They will be the winners in life. Just because someone is good at something doesn't mean that they have set goals or have stick-to-itiveness. You, young man, will go far because you will mature with the heart of your grandfather. And that is a great thing."

A tear came to her eye because she knew that at some point, Little Clint would replace his grandfather, and she hated to think of that moment but knew that Christmas Eve would be in good hands.

Chapter Sixty-Eight

"I have something else I would like to pass along to you," Big Clint said as they glazed out over to Dragon Mountain.

During your life, you will meet a lot of people. You will want all of them to become friends, but they are not true friends. During your life, you have to figure out a lot of things, and one is who will be your true friends throughout life."

"What do you mean?" Little Clint asked.

"People will want to be your friend," Big Clint said, "because you are a special person. But you will have experiences with people—some will be great, and some will be negative. When someone treats you poorly, you need to let them go and move on and find new friends, but always be true to your true friends."

"I think I understand," Little Clint replied. "When someone's bullying me or someone else, you want me to walk away and be nice to them but not let them into my circle of true friends again."

"Yes, be nice to everyone. You will only have a handful of true friend throughout your life. Your family will be your true friends. Maybe some friends from grade school, maybe some from high school, and even college. But your friends will change through your life, but you will have a core group of real friends that love you no matter what happens or how much money you make.

"I just want you to realize that the word *friend* is used very freely, but a true friend is hard to find. Once you find them, you will know it. Don't just throw them away. Appreciate what you have.

"You don't have to speak to them every day. You might not speak to them for ten years, and then when you see each other, it is like no time has passed, and you are right back where you left off."

"I think I understand, but it is something that I will learn as I mature," Little Clint said.

"You're wise beyond your years. I don't think I need to worry," his grandfather said as he leaned back and looked over at Dragon Mountain. "I don't think I need to worry about you."

CHAPTER SIXTY-NINE

They were enjoying their coffee when suddenly Thelma heard a loud moaning sound coming from the cottage. She jumped from her seat, spilling her coffee and tipping over her muffin in the process. "What's that noise?"

"I don't know. I don't hear anything," Stella said.

Thelma ran into the cottage and saw that her clear crystal ball was filled with colors and was making a low, dull moaning sound.

"My goodness. My goodness," Thelma kept saying under her breath as she looked into the crystal ball.

Stella walked into the room, and she did not hear anything. The crystal ball was just a clear piece of glass in her eyes.

"There's water…a blue sky…" Thelma explained to Stella what she was seeing in the crystal ball.

"Now the sky is turning bright red. The water is turning red. Oh my…"

Stella still could only see a clear ball.

"Oh. Oh. A creature like a sea serpent is coming out of the water," Thelma's voice cracked and became higher and more excited.

"What's happening now?" Stella asked.

"The serpent is going onto land," Thelma replied.

Stella watched as the crystal ball went completely black, and she heard the ball groan.

"What's happening?" Stella asked, panic evident in her voice.

Suddenly the crystal ball cracked internally.

The two women stood there and just stared in disbelief.

There was a louder moan, and then the crystal ball shattered into tiny pieced all over the table and floor.

"I've never heard of that happening to a crystal ball before," Thelma said sadly. "That must be an omen."

"Omen for what? For whom? What's going on?"

"I don't know, but I don't thinks it's good," Thelma replied.

Thelma retrieved her pink bowling ball bag and started placing the crystal pieces into the bag. Her hands were trembling.

"What's wrong?" Stella asked.

"Something is going to happen, and we have been foretold. But I don't know who to warn or who to help," Thelma said as she closed the bowling ball bag and just looked at the table where the crystal ball had spent its last summer vacation.

CHAPTER SEVENTY

Helga was hanging laundry outdoors on the clothesline. She pulled down the line to hang a sheet, and on the other side of the sheet were the two figures that had recently visited her.

"Nice day to dry sheets," the figure in gold said. "Let me introduce ourselves because we will be friends soon. I am Yang Yang, and this is Yin Yin."

They both bowed to Helga.

"I asked you to leave me alone," Helga said. "You are disturbing my family."

"We are here to kill the dragon that lives in this pond, and you will help us today even if we have to put you in a trance," Yin Yin said in a very authoritarian voice.

" We will explain to you our plans and your part in this plan," Yang Yang said.

Helga let go of the clothesline, and the sheets fluttered in the breeze.

Yin Yin and Yang Yang walked around the sheets and took Helga by her hands and led her to the steps of the camp.

In a trance, Helga sat down, and they explained their plans to her in great detail.

As they finished telling her the details, Yang Yang said, "You will get the old fat man on the field at the pavilion, and we will take it from there."

"Now get ready to go to the pavilion field," Yin Yin said.

Helga stood up and entered her camp in a trance. Her eyes were glassy, and her breathing was deep and slow. She reappeared in a couple of minutes, and she headed to the pavilion as if it was the only thing that she had to do in the world.

"She is under our spell. Now we will get the dragon prize and become wealthy and powerful," Yang Yang said as they followed Helga to the field at the pavilion.

CHAPTER SEVENTY-ONE

Yin Yin and Yang Yang had pulled a broken-down wagon from the shed on the pavilion's grounds and placed it in the middle of the small field. The spokes of one of the wagon wheels were broken, and that corner of the wagon drooped to the ground.

"You need to lay down under the wagon wheel, Helga," Yin Yin said, "and start yelling for help. When someone responds, tell them to get Big Clint to pull the wagon off you."

"Tell them to stay away," Yang Yang said. "Tell them that Big Clint will take care of everything."

Yin Yin and Yang Yang left Helga and hid in the bushes and waited.

Helga lay on the ground under the wagon and started yelling for help.

"Now what's that noise," Thelma said as she put the bowling ball bag into her bedroom.

"Someone is screaming for help," Stella said.

They ran out onto the deck and could see Helga laying under the wagon as if she was being crushed to death.

"Help! Help! Get Big Clint!" Helga yelled.

Thelma yelled back, "We will get him! Don't worry we will be there in a minute."

"No, only Big Clint. You stay where you are. You can't come over here, it's too dangerous!" Helga yelled back accentuating her yelling with a loud moan.

Stella ran to get Big Clint.

Big Clint was cleaning his shed when Stella called to him and told him what was happening.

Big Clint grabbed his work gloves, and he ran ahead of Stella to the pavilion.

Big Clint approached Helga, and as he was about to pull the wagon off her, Yin Yin and Yang Yang appeared out of the bushed with ropes in their hands.

Yin Yin grabbed Big Clint from behind and held his hand together while Yang Yang tied them.

"Old man, you are going to get the dragon out of the pond for us," Yang Yang said.

Helga crawled out from under the wagon.

"I thought that you were pinned by the wheel," Big Clint said.

"No, we are here to use you as bait to get the dragon out of the pond," Helga said in a low, slow voice.

"Helga, are you all right?" Big Clint asked because she was not acting herself.

"You will bring that dragon to me," Helga said directly to Big Clint with blank-looking eyes.

Yin Yin and Yang Yang grabbed Big Clint by his shoulders and his feet and put him into the wagon.

Helga picked up the ropes and tied Big Clint to the seat.

"Now start yelling for help," Helga said. "We will wait for the dragon."

Yin Yin took out a can from the rear of the wagon, and he started pouring gunpowder into the wagon, down the wooden wheels around and around the wagon making larger and larger circles. He walked toward the edge of the pond, leaving a trail of gunpowder.

"You have twenty-seven minutes from when I strike the match to get the dragon out of the water," Yang Yang said. "When he is dead, we will put out the fire, and you will be alive for another day.

If the dragon does not appear, you will burn like a marshmallow."

"Help! Help! Help!" Big Clint started yelling, but there was no sign of Timmy.

"Helga, will you do the pleasure of striking the match," Yang Yang said.

Helga and Yang Yang joined Yin Yin by the water's edge. Helga took a match from the matchbox and struck it against the rough surface of the box. The match tip turned bright blue, and she dropped the lit match onto the gunpowder.

CHAPTER SEVENTY-TWO

Yin Yin, Yang Yang and Helga were looking toward Dragon Mountain, but no dragon head came to the surface of the pond. Not even a ripple of any activity under the water. No signs of any life swimming, walking, or crawling under the water's surface. But the fire was still burning, the gun power creeping toward Big Clint.

"Help, someone help me!" Big Clint tried to scream, but the ropes were bound so tight that he could barely breathe.

The water slowly turned to a brilliant red color, and Yin Yin thought that it was the blood of the dragon in the pond. The sky turned the same color red as the pond.

Between the three peaks south of Colvin Hill, four fire-breathing dragons soared through the valleys. They were Timmy's mother, father, grandmother, and grandfather. They knew that dragon slayers had plans to kill their son today, and they were there to save Timmy.

"Quick, Helga! Become the dragon slayer you were meant to be," Yang Yang said.

Helga, appearing to still be under their spell, started to spin like a tornado, and when she stopped, she was dressed in a scarlet-red silk robe decorated with an embroidered dragon on her back with a dagger through its heart. There were gold dragon-embossed button on the front and more embroidery in the front and down the sleeves.

In her hand, Helga held a katana sword. The handle fit perfectly in her hand as if it was made for her. She looked down at her hand and braided into the leather handle were the words Ag Leh—Dragon Slayer.

Ag Leh. Who is Ag Leh? she thought. Then she realized that Ag Leh is Helga spelled backward. She realized she was once destined to become a dragon slayer.

The sunlight sparkled off the blade, and she glanced at the blade. Her reflection was that of a Chinese woman with blue-black hair. She paused, but then the blade revealed that the dragons were alarmingly close to her and the other dragon slayers.

Yin Yin, Yang Yang, and Helga all drew their katana swords; they were ready for the fight of their lives. This was the chance for Yin Yin and Yang Yang to become the world's most wealthy and most powerful men.

Timmy swam from the safety of his underwater cave, followed by all his pond friends. He told them to all stay under the water and not to attempt to be heroes.

Timmy stepped up onto the bank of the pond behind Helga.

"Helga, remember the dragon's blind spot. Remember the chart," Yin Yin screamed. "Get in position to spear his heart. Remember the blind spot."

She recalled an image of a wall chart with a dragon and a drawn-in triangle showing the place to stand so the monster could not see her. Helga quickly ran around Timmy, placing herself behind his left elbow next to his wing.

Timmy also moved quickly, so Helga had to keep dodging his wings and his tail. Timmy's tail almost sent Helga into the pond.

Timmy' parents charged toward Yin Yin and Yang Yang, and they too had to dodge the onslaught of talons, teeth, wings, and fire. Timmy's grand-parents stayed back, surveying the fight, ready to attack if they were needed.

Timmy's grandfather saw Big Clint tied up in the wagon, and he flew down, scaring Big Clint half to death. Big Clint was sure that the dragon was going to destroy him, but the dragon stopped beside the wagon and, with his flame, burned the ropes that bound Big Clint.

Big Clint ran with all his might toward the safety of the pavilion as the dragon threw a flame at the wagon and with a thunderous boom, the wagon, with all the gunpowder, went up in flames.

Helga continued to try and stay in Timmy's blind spot, but he moved so fast that it seemed impossible to find the blind spot.

Timmy's mother spun around in the air, and her tail sent Yang Yang sailing into the pond. Yang Yang sputtered and swam back to shore. He was after the blood, heart, and horns of the dragon that he pursued for so many years.

Timmy's father hovered over Yin Yin. Yin Yin looked up with fear and saw the underbelly of the largest creature he had ever imagined. He could smell the scent of this creature. He could smell the methane from the fire the monster was exhaling. The dragon's talons scraped his back and tore his robe. The dragon's tail hit him, and Yin Yin grabbed on and was flung back and forth until he lost his grip.

Helga threw her arms out and spun herself around and once again looked like a tornado. When she stopped, she looked more powerful and stronger. She took in a deep breath, and she popped the buttons off of her robe. They went flying into the grass and one of the dragons stepped on them, pushing them into the ground.

Helga decided that it was now or never; she lunged toward Timmy with her arm fully expended holding the katana sword aimed at Timmy's heart. Timmy dropped to the ground, and Helga flew over his head and the back of her robe caught on Timmy's horn. Helga hung in midair, legs and arms flailing.

Timmy's mother flew over to protect her only offspring, and she blew a flame at Helga. The flame singed Helga robe, and it burned the skin of her upper arm in the design of a dragon. This was Timmy's mother's way of marking her enemy.

Helga's robe ripped, and she fell to the ground with a thud. Helga felt defeated, and she was exhausted.

Yin Yin and Yang Yang ran to the pavilion, hoping to take Big Clint as a hostage, but Timmy's grandparents each grabbed one of the dragon slayers by the collars of their robes and flew toward the mountain range that they had flown through. The dragons were going to take the dragon slayers to the mutton fat jade mine in China and imprison them behind the metal bars in the main room of the mine.

The prison had never been used but will be the final place that Yin Yin and Yang Yang will ever see until they die of natural causes. They will be within reach of the most valuable jade in the world but will not be able to touch it.

Timmy's mother stood over Helga, holding Helga's robe with her talon, knowing that she was not going anywhere. Timmy walked over to his mother, and they wrapped their neck around each, which is a dragon form of a human hug.

Timmy's father walked over to his son and gave him the dragon hug. Timmy had not seen his family in many years, and he was so happy to see them.

Helga lay on the ground afraid that she was going to be stepped on.

Timmy's pond friends all showed their head above the surface of the pond. Mica was thrilled to see Timmy and his parent, and she watched Timmy's grandparents fly away, carrying two figures in robes.

All the animals of the pond and around the pond watched the emotional meeting of their friend Timmy and his family.

It was time for Timmy's parents to leave because they had to guard the mutton fat jade mine, so they said their good-byes, and they spread their wings and flew toward the triple peaks south of Colvin Hill.

As they flew off, they turned around and flew over Tinmouth Pond as a goodwill pass and to impress Timmy's friends, and then they flew south toward the peaks and then on to China.

CHAPTER SEVENTY-THREE

Timmy retreated to the safety of Tinmouth Pond, and he had stories to tell all his friends.

Helga slowly composed herself, and the scarlet robe had changed back into her housedress. The katana sword was gone too. She was exhausted and confused.

Big Clint came out of the pavilion and walked over to Helga. The burn mark on Helga's arm and the last remaining pieces of the wagon scattered around the field were the only reminders of the dragon fight. He too was confused. He helped Helga to her feet, and he walked her home.

Helga felt a tingle on her arm, and she looked down at the burn mark in the shape of a dragon. *Where did that come from?* she thought as she scratched it, thinking it was just dirt, but she realized that it was a permanent mark that would be controlling her outburst and negative thoughts.

Not a word was spoken between Helga and Big Clint because they did not know if what had just happened was reality or a bad nightmare.

Big Clint got Helga home, and then he walked home. When he got home, he hugged his wife and his grandson like there was no tomorrow as soon as he walked through the screen door.

Big Clint was alive and happy.

CHAPTER SEVENTY-FOUR

Big Clint was sitting in his truck tooting the horn, trying to prod Stella and Thelma along. He had to get them to the train within an hour, or they would miss the first leg of their journey home.

The two ladies came out of the cottage with their bags in hand. Big Clint jumped out of the truck and loaded the bags into the bed of the truck.

"What's that tinkling sound in the bowling bag," Big Clint asked.

"My crystal ball had an accident," Thelma said. "There was a vision of the sky and water turning bright red and a sea serpent walking out of the water. Then the crystal ball went black and then exploded. I think it was an omen, but I'm not sure of what."

Big Clint helped the ladies into the cab of the truck, and he got into the driver's seat.

As he drove down the road, he asked if the ladies had a great vacation.

Stella said she had the best time ever and that they were all ready making plans for next summer at Tinmouth Pond.

Big Clint thought about the water and sky turning red and a creature as an omen. He was the only person who knew the secret that it really was an omen, but he could never tell them.

The old truck traveled to Rutland; the Southern ladies were delivered to the train platform.

Big Clint unloaded their bags and gave a big hug to Stella and Thelma and handed their bags to the porter.

Thelma and Stella boarded the train; and as the train left the station, the ladies waved to Big Clint out of the window, and he waved back, wishing them a safe journey home.

CHAPTER SEVENTY-FIVE

"Look Hun," Chris's mother said. "We have a text from our kid."

> Dear Mom and Dad, I won the Pulitzer Prize for my Chinese jade mine article. Thank you for everything! Love, Chris.

"We did a great job raising that one," Chris's father replied with a smile.